In

the

Same

Breath

In the Same Breath

Edited by representatives

from

Inishfree Writers

and

Newtownabbey Writers' Group

In the Same Breath
published November 1998

written and edited by
Inishfree Writers
and
Newtownabbey Writers' Group,
with funding from
The East Meets West Project
administered by
Co-operation North

Photographic Plates
© Royce Harper

Many thanks
to the staff of
Newtownabbey Borough Council
who were involved in the project,
and to the Management Team of
The East Meets West Project

Cover
'Celtic Dance' by Brian Mullan
© Newtownabbey Borough Council

Back cover
'In the Same Breath' by Maureen Browne
© The East Meets West Project

Typeset by AZ-Tech

ISBN 0 9534597 0 5

Introduction

The Chimney Corner Hotel sits on the side of the road to Antrim town, about two miles from the Newtownabbey village of Carnmoney, which is swallowed now in the urban grasp of Glengormley, six or eight miles from the sprawl of Belfast city on the shores of Belfast Lough. The lough itself runs ten or so miles down the coast to the small town of Carrickfergus and laps around the Norman ramparts of Carrick Castle where William of Orange landed in 1690 before marching inland to his historic encounter with James II at the River Boyne. It begins to widen here, into the North Channel, spreading out to separate the shores of Scotland from the breathtaking grandeur of the Antrim Coast Road.

On its way to Ballycastle, the road writhes along the water's edge, through Glenarm to Cushendun and Cushendall and if you cared to turn west here you would find yourself surrounded by the serene beauty of the Glens of Antrim and you would hear the rush of peat-stained mountain water over the rocks at Glenarif. But if you allowed your nose to lead you and kept heading north you would catch a smell other than the salty sea breeze.

Built on the banks of the Bush river from which it takes its name, the Bushmills distillery is the oldest of its kind in the world. You can, if you wish, for a small consideration, be led on a tour of the premises and see for yourself the birthplace of the famous, world-revered Black Bush whiskey. And sample it too, if you're curious. Purely in the interests of research, of course, to see what all the fuss is about.

Long before it became a hotel, the Chimney Corner was a hostelry, a post stop, catering to the mail coaches and wayfarers on the Antrim line, a welcome opportunity, while the horses were changed, to refresh a parched throat and relieve the dusty tedium of the long, bone-jarring excursion to Derry or Coleraine or down the coast to the bustling market town of Ballycastle.

Highwaymen plied their trade here. Brigands stalked the lonely roads. And for their sins many a one of them kicked their heels on the gallows at Greenisland.

Travellers are safe now from the highwayman and the footpad. They can come in confidence to Newtownabbey. And they do. They come from America and France and Italy and England, from Germany, Africa, Canada and from Australia.

One Friday in June they came from closer to home. Travelling from an island three miles off the Atlantic coast of Donegal — Inishfree.

It had begun a month ago in May with a series of phone calls.

As part of the East Meets West project to promote peace and reconciliation throughout the island of Ireland, the idea was the long-cherished notion of Cathy Cole, Leisure Development Officer of Arts for Newtownabbey Council.

Gather the most talented writers in the area, mould them into a group and give them a purpose. Formed initially from a core of ten writers from the Newtownabbey area the group would create a working relationship with similar groups in Donegal. They would exchange knowledge, swap information and ideas, promote a greater awareness and appreciation of the huge diversity and wealth of cultural and traditional heritage that exists on both sides of the border.

The initial meeting of the Newtownabbey writers with their Inishfree counterparts took place in The Chimney Corner Hotel, Newtown-abbey. They shook hands and introduced themselves and made ice-breaking cracks. They talked and laughed easily, the way people from our country do when they get together. They had a meeting then, throwing suggestions around, exploring the possibilities that this gathering was revealing. Cathy Cole outlined the plan.

'I want a book,' she said. 'A joint publication. A compilation of the best works of all the people here. A book to celebrate our historical and cultural differences and highlight the things we have in common. We will be funded by Co-operation North — and we have until December.'

The ideas tumbled into the room. A book of what? Poetry? Prose? Humour? Adventure? Romance? History? All of this. But what else? Someone said, why not a CD? Music, maybe. But, who would buy it? Where do we sell it? Endless possibilities.

The meeting broke up with the announcement of dinner but the enthusiastic discussion continued over the excellent fare.

After dinner the real *craic* began. The visitors regaled us with entertaining readings of their work, the writers from Newtownabbey reading theirs in return.

The result was like a mini-festival in itself. The variety and standard of the material left no-one in any doubt. Here was a book waiting to be published. Not only a book, but for the blind and visually impaired perhaps a CD too, with poets and writers of prose reading from their own work. Maybe professional readers, musicians too. It was like a welling fountain of untapped resource. The reality began to take shape.

A return invitation was issued to the Newtownabbey Group to attend the forthcoming annual Festival in Inishfree. They would go on August twenty-first. Down to Dungloe and across by boat to the little island of Inishfree. There, among the grey abandoned homes of those who once lived there, they would be welcomed into the lively homes of those who still did. They would join in their *Siamsa* and follow the piper in the Blessing of the Roads. They would listen to the poetry and tap their feet to the music. They would talk and laugh and they would make good friends. West had met East. Now East would meet West.

This book is the child of those meetings.

Gerry McAuley
Newtownabbey Writers' Group

Illustrations   Plates

Heritage

All praise to you dear Inishfree,
Our lonely island home;
As home to us you'll always be
However far we roam.
When childhood scenes we had to leave,
Our bread and livelihood to learn;
On alien shores we'd oft-times grieve,
And to return some day we'd yearn.
But life with all its turns and twists,
For us decided otherwise;
New homes were made and families raised
Beneath these other foreign skies.

Dark days then came when your proud name
Was often sullied without cause,
As strangers roamed o'er your terrain
With scant respect for rules or laws.
Now, God be praised, again you're raised,
Like the fabled Phoenix, proud and tall,
To take your rightful place again
On the Rosses coast of Donegal.
Now kind and caring thoughtful folk,
Who tend your homes with care and love,
Will raise your status and esteem
And all your troubles rise above.

In future years we hope to see
Your friendly lights shine out once more
Across the waves of Boylagh Bay
From far Glen Head to Arranmore.
Peace and prosperity we hope,
May be your lot in years to come.,
As the march of time propels us on
Towards the new millennium.
While age and traumas take their toll
That date we may not live to see,
But we hope descendants, yet unborn,
Will inherit our love for Inishfree

Aunty Cathie's Esperanto

*M*ost of us can identify an Aunty Cathie from some phase of our lives. Though long-since gone, our Aunty Cathie's unique VOCK-A-BUILLIARY, which gave us so much amusement in the past, still surfaces at times to keep her memory alive.

She was always 'ON THE HORNS OF A DILLIMA' over some problem and, like most of us, could show annoyance when 'THE WEAN'SES FITBAW BAW' was kicked over her fence and through her garden.

Rising prices were another abomination to her, complaining that, once she'd paid her 'ELECTRITICITY' bill and the weekly 'MESSINGES' there was only enough left to get her man 'HAUF A PAIR OF PYJAMASES' which he was 'awfy sair needin'. His last pair were from the STARVATION ARMY jumble sale and didn't wear all that well.

A lot of Cathie's financial difficulties were blamed on the government — 'Thae high heid yins' with an earlier Prime Minister getting his share of the stick: 'THAT HARLOT McMILLAN SHOULD BE BANISHED FROM THE FACE OF THIS EARTH.' At election time a canvasser who appeared at Cathie's door, clad in a 'STIMULATED SHEEPSKIN' coat was sent packing with a flea in his ear. To escape the brunt of Cathie's tirade he fled down the path as if he were 'JET REPELLED'.

Despite her cash difficulties, Cathie's charity box was always included in the budget and no reasonable appeal was ever denied. The 'Thalidomide' disaster gave her great cause for concern — 'THON POOR WEE THALDOLOMIDE WEANS NEED ALL THE HELP THEY CAN GET'.

The visit of Cathie's niece from Chicago was one of the highlights of her final years. She described to us in detail the fashionable outfit the visitor wore, with long 'REPELS' in a 'CONTRACTING' colour. She wished we could have seen it for ourselves as she just couldn' 'PRE-SCRIBE' it properly, but she was full of praise for the hotel up town in which her niece entertained her, pronouncing the meal 'PURE DEL-E-

O-SHIOUS', and what that chef could do with just the addition of some 'DISSAPATED' coconut was a marvel.

If Aunty Cathie were alive today her comments on Royalty would be very interesting. She had an avid interest in all their affairs and indiscretions. In relating the matrimonial tangles of one Royal person-age she told us how, to escape some scandal, he was married off to someone the public called 'June the Dancer' and she assured us 'AYE, AN YE CAN BE SHAIR THAT WIS YIN MARRIAGE THAT WIS NEVER CONSTIPATED'.

Her lively conversation was always peppered with words like HACKITT, CHIPPIT, SOMEONE WHO WAS ATTIKIT, OR, in an extreme case, 'A PUIR SOUIL WHO DRAPPIT DOON DEID JIGGINS' at the pensioners' social.

Aunty Cathie was brought to mind again on a recent visit to one of the islands. The waitress in our hotel, bemoaning the weather and its effect on the ferry timetable, causing frequent disruption, told us, 'Oh for the past month that ferry has been very 'erotic'.

Cathie's passing has left a big void in our lives. She will be quoted and remembered when most of us have passed on without trace.

Learning

*E*dumacation! It's such an absorbing subject!

Our sojourn here in the University of Life teaches us more than can be learnt from text books in any sophisticated educational establishment. From the cradle to the grave we are always learning.

With the latent talent inherent in all of us we owe it to ourselves to develop and endeavour to attain our full potential, bearing in mind that rigid thinking and fixed ideas are the enemies of personal development and, trying to please everybody is the never-fail recipe for failure.

Phrases and dialects peculiar to one area can be a complete enigma to someone from a different background or country. Equally, unfamiliar words can also cause a degree of consternation.

It was over fifty years ago that I first heard the word 'phlebitis'. Endeavouring to conceal my embarrassment by pretending that I hadn't heard, I was dismayed that anyone could speak openly on such a subject. My God! You'd think that anyone who knew that they had *fleas* in the house would try to keep the knowledge secret; yet here was she, a woman from a clean, decent, respectable family, admitting to having been flea-bitten, even to the extent of requiring hospital treatment! What a mess! The mind boggles — whatever that may mean. There must have been myriads of fleas to have inflicted such injury. Some poor nurses really do need our sympathy.

Then there was the day when 'A nest of young rats' was brought up in conversation. This brought a nudge from an equally unenlightened companion, with the comment: "Did you hear that? 'A nest of young rats?' Don't they know the difference? Rats don't have young. It's the mice who breed and then their young grow to rathood." And so it goes on.

Auld Jamie, away from home for the first time in his life, was finding his stay in hospital particularly tedious. After a lifetime of being accustomed to tea so strong it could be sliced, he was finding the hospital fare not quite so appetising. At home his tea was always served in a bowl (pronounced 'boul') which kept it hot to the last mouthful and, because of the size of this receptacle, dispensed with this necessity of refilling. He wasn't at all happy with cup and saucer, and the second cup never tasted quite like the first. Not that the taste of the first was to his liking either.

He was also having difficulty with some of the medical terminology and the questions he struggled to answer. A young nurse, filling in her report sheet asked: 'How is your head today, Jamie? Are you still feeling a bit dizzy? Did your bowels move this morning?' She was more than a bit nonplussed when Jamie exploded:

"BOULS IS IT? Sure I haven't seen a decent boul since they tuk me in here, whoever moved them. All I get is just one of them silly wee things with a loop on the side of it and a wee plate under it that's not even big enough for feeding the cat. And that slush that's in it is enough to put any poor man's head into a right *buarach agus fosta, níl me ábaltá rud ar bíth* — AAGH — *THOSGUGH ORAIBH UILIG.*"

Unable to express himself adequately in this unfamiliar lingo, he'd lapsed into his native tongue, leaving his listeners 'fair furfoken'.

Aye indeed , this *edumacation* is a great thing when you can get the hang of it.

Norah Eagleson
Inishfree Writers

North by Northwest

In the north
appearances are deceptive.
Electrified shops full of smiling white teeth
selling polished half truths,
washing our dirty linen in public
excuses for ethical cleansing.

Westerly winds bring relations closer
cousins twice removed,
black mouthing each other.
Cutting nails right down
to the quick and the dead,
shaking a stick at God and the Devil.

The city simmers,
a voluptuous lady all tits and thighs
smoking like a trooper,
through three hundred drunken years.
Held down by contradictions
legs waving in salty communion
raped upon history's ferocious bed.

Beneath a waning moon
something in-between stirs,
the hound of Ulster, takes head staggers
wears his reversible dog collar,
savaged by ancestral tongues.
Howling his last howl
barks madly into the future.

The Piper

From behind glass he conjures silent music
hardly seen by people passing,
fingers move upon the chanter
casting spells for those who have ears,
outside Rosemary Street Presbyterian.

Shadow railings lilt to his tune
under the classical balustrade
citizens engage in the lunch time tango,
as the piper at the gates
of the millennium,
taps his foot to keep the political rhythm.

Equality, Liberty, Fraternity,
the tarnished sunlight of two hundred years
can unite disunited Irishmen,
speaking for everyone
with its beautiful ideas.
Engrossed, self absorbed,
a moment's silence
to twist the regulator,
fine tuning to get the right sound.

Tossing him a coin,
music of opposites
the flats and sharps
stays in my head all day.
Finding a sweet concordance of melody
the city hums along,
My Lagan Love
lost in time and distance.

When the piper leaves
his shadow, reluctant to go,
plays on,
plays on.

Blood Brothers

A population takes lessons in forgiveness
as the statelet ramshackles on,
some play truant
learning assassinating words.
Release the grey giants
that trample through a nation's mind,
remembering every indiscretion.

Only the tips of icebergs show
testing the specific gravity
ratio of hate, weight,
to a given volume.
Misconceptions multiply
in the fourth hand bookshop,
a yellowed poster advertises
Harry Houdini's life story.

He performs the great trick
breaking free of handcuffs and chains,
live after death.
Seeing beyond the present
the need to practise escapology.

Symposium

Finding myself at the world's end
in the company of writers
who silver tongued their way
through sun and rain.
Here if you shake a tree
a thousand words
come falling down,
pulling feathery parodies
from poets' mouths
to tickle cloudy ears.
Hear the echo of angels' laughter
they sing much older songs
out on love's edge
soothing aged hearts.

Again myself finding
at the world's beginning,
knee deep in similes
and smart metaphors,
which clutter up Sunday
when even God rested.
I swept them all away,
leaving clever phrases
half-finished continents, and creatures,
and four-legged men and women
before he thought of horses,
sticking in the bristles
like dog hairs,
like the Donegal kindness perhaps.
Newly created weather
takes a turn for the better,
softly raining poems.

Waking the nimble big cats
that paw and claw and rip
at the fabric of thought.

Swallowtail

Why do taxi drivers
always have swallows
tattooed on their arms?
Maybe in September
they'll tug under the skin
trying to escape human bondage,
the pull of brothers and sisters
difficult to resist.

Perhaps that's why
we have so many
one armed taxi drivers in Belfast.
If only cabs
had feathers and wings,
taxis would fly south in the winter
with or without their drivers.

Her Birthday

Lingering on Macedon Point
ships leave little scars
characters rip paper water.
Single elm tree fingered her slightly foxed pages,
she spoke of cats, commitment, and babies,
he spoke of poetry, summer heat,
and about a woman who passed wearing yellow shoes,
honing his Irish evasiveness.
He picked up clay that was chalk
drew a circle without hands
her clock ticking.

Linear metropolis glows obliquely
catches itself on,
transistors receiving late light waves.
Tuning into English radio
she always liked the BBC,
listening to her mother's anguish
from emerald through Wight isle,
a birth in the ionosphere.

Inside the Mini Cooper
eye words painted evenings warm minutes,
she fell asleep across steering wheel.
Half closed lunar eyelid napped,
opened mussel shell glinted.
Outside prolific static gave enlightenment.

They lay in clammy terracotta rooms
baking skin suits glazing over,
immured by night's kiln.
They blazed between day and day,
the plenitude of ash
blackened sheets,
love's wonderful scarlatina.

Sumo

His girlfriend
challenges his perception of female beauty,
she used to be cruelly thin
now she is big, fat, and proud.
He thought of those voluptuous women
lounging about in Ruben's paintings.
Well he knows
their food bill has rocketed
but he will enjoy the trip to Japan.
Breaking those ancient taboos
the first Irish person
to compete in a Basho.

Even more shocking, a woman,
displaying her womanliness!

Prophesy

For Kirsten

In February world's sleep late
mornings new hammer
planishing the copper sun.
On a hill of prophesy
ice fingers clenched water
held overnight for questioning,
crystal bones crack
under muscle pressure.
Rested in a field of spiders
that spun skeins of dreams,
performing high wire tricks
a million acrobats
flying on nothingness.

Mutation began,
it was the four eyes
and eight legs each
that caused some difficulty.
Nature's course was fixed,
having a hundred babies at the first go.
We lived on flies, air, and sunshine,
together making ever more beautiful webs,
which caught thunder clouds
and love's lightning.

She began to change slowly
back to her old self,
only leaving a shy smile
she departed the webscape.
Six months later,
he folded his returned
letters and envelopes into paper ships.
Set sail, along with his thousand grandchildren
across the big pond,
looking for his mate
overcame his humanophobia.

First Snow

For Aaron, Laura, Hannah, and Katie

Appreciating the crystal catalyst of time,
scanning cosy settees of cloud
being re-upholstered with snow.
A winter desert grows in car parks
unblemished paper newly made
settles down layer on layer.
Spelling out names proves irresistible,
collected glinting diamonds
that disappeared on contact,
the laughter they shared.
The child fits inside his uncle's shoe
lives and footprints crisscross
days of simplicity and happiness recalled.

Tissue tingles under surface
burning coldness reddens fingers,
magnetic whiteness used its powerful attraction
pulls hands into freezing dimensions.
In from the cold
the boy, and man, and the child that walks within,
watched from ageless windows,
enchanted by wind driven sky dancers
street lit performance.
Light and heavy rhythms of falling flakes rhyme.

Telescopic

Through a telescope things seem closer,
spring rain congeals the politically incorrect dust
sweeping it under the newly laid carpet.
Quick sharp worded showers
glitter and glint menacingly,
the population slip, slip, slips away unseen
sleeping water reflects another side.

Grandeur's disarticulated body
observed in a thousand windows.
Night's metamorphosis creeps on apace,
buildings evolve, become creatures
take on fresh animal identities,
only alive for an evening.
The Linenopolis moving in streetscapes
sinking into damask dreams.

Everything seems further away than ever
humanity is made of light and shadow,
through a lens or glass darkly
feeling the chemistry of the possible.

Heat

Citizens grilled themselves momentarily
into flags of every complexion,
pigments darken absorb combustion
producing archipelagoes across turbulent seas.
Clenched fists and bloody palms
sweating certainties
mop the same brow,
life in the chromosphere.

Unprejudiced light showers everyone
invisible x-rays show structural faults,
develop negative and positive photographs on footpaths.
Nothing is ever black or white
gasping shadows seek greyness,
exposure to a different heat
looking for cloud
tolerance glistening,
Ireland after the rain.

Iain Campbell Webb
Newtownabbey Writers' Group

Generationen

— an maine Tochter —

Kaum kann ich's fassen
ist sie schon da
die Zeit
dich zu lassen?
Wo du gerade jetzt
mich vor emen Spiegel setzt!
Wie gerne flippte ich aus
tät's auch gern jetzt.
Wie geme fühlte ich das Leben
aufleben!
Doch du schaust aus dem
    Spiegel,
weist mich in Schranken,
zeigst mir den Platz,
— das ist es was schmerzt!
Daß ich nicht kann mit dir,
die ich liebe,
kann lachen
kann weinen
die Welt ergründen
die Jugend fühlen?
Andere Bande sind es
die uns binden.
Dies zu erkennen,
neu zu entdecken
ist nun an mir.
Und er wird mir klar,
main Platz
im Reigen der Generationen.

Generations

— to my daughter —

Hardly I can believe it
it's already there —
the time
to let you go?
Where you just now
put me in front of a mirror!
How I had liked to flip out,
I'd like to do it now, too.
How I'd like to feel life
renew in me!
However you look out of the
    mirror
you put me in frames,
you show me my place
— that is what hurts!
That I can't
laugh —
cry — with you
who I love
discover the world
feel the youth?
There are other links
which bind us.
To recognise this
to rediscover this
is now up to me.
And I become aware
of my place
in the sequel of generations.

Heidi Schulz
Inishfree Writers

34

Ballad of the Back and Forth

As you stumble down a country road
In an alcoholic haze
'Neath the foot of this purple mountain
Looming up into your gaze
The still night air is innocent
Ignoring this dark, unwholesome phase and
Home is where the heart aches, nearly there

Now the sound of trickling
Pours soft into your ears
A thin black brook is winding through
The dirt and dust of years
I see you veer toward, it, abandoning the path
That felt your rising anger and overflowing wrath
And home is where the heart aches, over there

Then you take a cupful of water to your face
Cooling down your temper
Reminding you of time and place
Thinking it's now or never in
The cripples' obstacle-race
As the birds sleep silent in the hedgerows

Go on, rustle up your straying herd
Of animal passions
The grass that's cropped too fine
Won't feed your insatiable hunger, no
Won't make a vintage wine
Unfurl your battle-streamers, spread out all your lime
Strip the ground of carrion, it's fighting time
And home is where the heart breaks, almost there

Take a walk through ghost-town
Past the stables and the mine
Keep your eyes peeled for the spirit
Who's selling divining-signs
Yes, yes the moon will kiss your cheek
As you step howling out of line
For home is where the heart aches entwine

There is someone burning forests
In your dark, reclusive mind
Smoking up your pupils, you're chewing at the rind
There's something in the acrid air
Something you can't find
Fear is growing stronger that you'll be left behind
I know your heart aches, it's laid bare

As you stride down these empty streets
With cold black slits for eyes
An old bent man wielding a crooked stick
Draws another long fine line
Across your mental border, oh
Your cup's still full of brine
Let your sheep go wandering
Wipe the dust from the shine

And yes, the moon will kiss your cheek
As you step howling out of line
Because for you
Home is where the heartaches combine.

Royce Harper
Newtownabbey Writers' Group

First Taste

*I*t was a warm, sunny July in 1963 that I was given my first taste of Donegal. I had not envisaged the reality of such beauty.

Many years before, at the age of fifteen, my husband Donal had left his home — Inishfree, a remote island, off the West coast of Donegal.

I had listened so often to a multitude of his stories. He told me about his family, his friends and relations, most of which I was hardly able to take in.

He told me about the cold winter's morning he set out to pick winkles, a job most men on the island did to supplement their income. That morning, reluctantly, he had trekked across the frosty island with his galvanised bucket. Taking his grumpy mood out on the innocent receptacle, he swung it to such an extent it almost flew out of his hand. Unable to make up his mind as to where he should pick, he took a coin from his pocket and tossed it into the air. Heads he would pick down at the shore or tails to keep closer to the land. The land won the toss, he would pick the winkles over at Inishinny. Inishinny is a tiny island within walking distance of Inishfree accessible only at low tide.

When the bucket was full he stooped to pick it up, by this time the handle was covered in frost. His hands already blue and aching with the cold, gripped the freezing metal handle which adhered to his hand. He had had enough — this was the final straw. He threw the bucket of dark grey winkles with all his might across the gravel that edged the salt water hole; his life would have to change, he could stand the confinements of island life no longer. He had to leave. In that moment of desperation, he made his decision; he would join his uncle John in Scotland. His mind made up, he returned home to tell his mother of his plans, promising that he would always help her out. Part of his promise was to send her most of his earnings. He would be missed. He was fully aware of her dependence on him to help keep the home running, it was he that milked the cows, brought home the turf, picked winkles for a few extra shillings and helped out at the fishing. Now it was down to her new husband and his younger brother and sisters.

Donal's mother, Bridget, was heartbroken at his decision. At his young age this was a monstrous idea, but she knew that it was inevitable and that it would be only a matter of time before he left, just as many of the other young men had left the island to look for work. It was no good trying to stop him either, so she gave him thirty pounds, and with her blessing he left the next morning with full intentions never to set foot on the island again. He was going to join his uncle and find work in Scotland. By the age of twenty Donal found his way to the small mining village of Crosskeys in South Wales where I lived. We met in our local Italian cafe, a meeting place for teenagers of the village. We married the following year.

In the summer of 1963 we took our first holiday together in Ireland. It was the first time Donal had been back since he had made his hasty departure for Scotland nine years before.

Apart from the occasional Sunday school outing I had travelled little. We decided to fly, something that was also new to me.

We boarded the plane at Cardiff Airport, with our new baby boy, and in less than an hour landed on Irish soil.

From the airport in Dublin we hired the cronkiest old car and travelled the endless journey to Dungloe in Co Donegal.

I was feeling apprehensive as we journeyed on through the Irish countryside, studded with stone edged fields and small cottages.

My primary concern was not on the journey itself or the strange unfamiliar roads, but rather the question of a constant supply of Ostermilk, or even Cow & Gate. Maybe Irish mothers fed their babies themselves and hadn't to rely on boxed dried milk as I did. There were so many maybe's running through my head. Exhausted, we landed in Dungloe, where Donal's mother welcomed us with open arms.

After Donal's sudden flight to foreign lands, Bridget and the remaining family had left Inishfree Island to enjoy life in a brand new council house in Dungloe with all mod cons.

After a day or two I became more accustomed to life in Donegal. I made many comparisons between this life and my own.

I was amazed to discover that only one large generator supplied the whole of Dungloe and surrounding area with electricity. There were very few televisions in existence, and I can still recall my horror when, turning on the tap, a stream of water poured forth as brown as the earth itself. How, I thought, could I be expected to bath my precious baby in water that colour!

If I thought Dungloe was a step back in time, then I was in for another surprise.

Donal came home one afternoon with the news that he had borrowed a boat, he would take me to Inishfree Island. His reasons for leaving in the first place gone and forgotten, his memory of life as a child were to remain humorously, happy times. Bridget was delighted to be asked to look after her new grandson for the day, she said it would give us some time to enjoy ourselves.

Donal was far more familiar with boats and island life than he was of the busy town of Dungloe.

Armed with a pair of oars, and rowlocks he set off over the pebbles with me trying to keep up the pace as he raced down to the small green boat that awaited us. Donal quickly untied the boat and motioned to me. I wasn't too sure of myself, but somehow managed to get into the boat as it tossed about from side to side. I had never been in a boat in my life.

To Donal it was second nature and I marvelled at the ease at which he manoeuvred the craft, and at the strength at which he rowed the little boat effortlessly through the waves, until we reached the shore of Inishfree.

There was no pier where we landed, only a large cluster of rocks that loomed high and slippery. I was extremely nervous at the thought of setting foot on them.

'I don't have to climb those rocks do I?' I asked, still trembling from the movement of the boat. He threw my frightened plea to the wind.

'It's easy. Just step on to it,' he said in his usual abrupt manner. Watching and waiting at the top of the jagged rock in the bright glare of the sun, stood an old woman clad in a long black skirt, a dark woollen shawl draped around her shoulders.

She smiled at me, with a wrinkled smile, her silver hair twisted loosely into a bun, sparkled in the sunlight. She took my hand and firmly announced, 'You're welcome,' then added 'a thousand welcomes'. She squeezed my hand so tight I thought she would stop the flow of blood.

'So this is your new wife, Donal,' she said. 'Isn't she the wee young thing, Donal.' I felt excluded from the conversation as she gave him her appraisal of his new but young wife.

Embarrassed, as to what she may say about him in my presence, Donal nodded, then walked on briskly in the direction of the old woman's house.

The old woman and I followed him, she nattering away to her heart's content whilst I struggled to keep up with her endless continuous questions. Where did I live? Were my parents still living? Did I have any brothers or sisters? How old were they? At last we reached the small but spacious, crofters cottage, set out neatly in a fenced garden. The old woman made me welcome, while Donal took up his usual place in the corner, as if it were only yesterday he had made the same simple moves. I was her guest. She bade me sit at the table. She would get us some tea.

I watched her every movement in disbelief. She lifted the heavy three legged pot filled with potatoes from the centre of the low smouldering fire, to make room for an equally heavy and enormous black kettle, that had been left simmering on one hob whilst on the other sat a heavy pan of fish.

I have to be in some kind of dream, I thought. If I pinch myself hard I might wake up. Or was I in some other world?

The old woman set me a place on the oilcloth covered table, and from the large dresser she carefully took down two white china mugs decorated with bands of green. She poured out the tea, then handed me the jug of milk.

'It's fresh from this morning's milking,' she assured me.

I poured the tiniest drop into the steaming tea, the rich smell of warm cream clung to my nostrils. Then, much to my dismay, she promptly took the jug from me and added more, stating she was not short of milk. Oh no, did she not have plenty.

I watched with interest as she cut into the scone of bread, baked in her pot oven over the fire, that very morning. Then handing me a slice, she confirmed that her supply of butter equalled that of the milk, and offered me the butter dish.

'Don't be afraid, lass, eat your fill.'

She smiled at me — a kind, toothless smile.

The old woman continued to question me, was I able to sew, could I darn a pair of socks, and — most importantly — could I cook?

Then suddenly from the corner of my eye, I thought I saw a pair of man's legs that looked for all the world as if they were tightly bandaged, emerge from behind pink flowery curtains that hung along side the kitchen fire. On closer inspection I could see he was wearing woollen longjohns. I was certain I wasn't imagining things, but was afraid to stare for fear of upsetting him. Then the top half of the man appeared.

I was soon to discover the man, the old woman's husband, was only getting up, and the pretty curtains concealed a kitchen bed.

'He often rises late these days,' she offered as an explanation.

The man was far less surprised at finding me in his kitchen, than I was at the strange sight I had of him, flinging his legs out of his kitchen bed at the side of the fire.

It was time to leave them, that kindly old pair, to visit the remaining thirty houses on Inishfree. At each house our visit was received with the same overwhelming welcome.

Donal's uncle John (John Billy John) was not at home, we had missed him. The name intrigued me, until I had the full interpretation. John was his Grandfather's name, Billy his Father's name, and his own name John. It was difficult for me to understand but then, we also had names in Wales that sounded strange to other people, for instance, there was Jones the milk, Evans the oil, and Berti Williams the coal. Uncle John (BJ) had gone to the mainland for his messages and was not expected back until late in the evening, every neighbour informed us. We were disappointed. It was Donal's idea of an unexpected pleasant surprise for his uncle, instead of the many unpleasant ones he and friends had bestowed upon him over the years. I did not have the pleasure of meeting uncle John this time, neither were we able to return to the island this holiday, for the weather turned stormy. Uncle John would have to wait until next time.

From that day on, Inishfree Island was firmly planted in my memory. A happy contented place where the welcome was immeasurable. Inishfree — a tiny remnant of earth time had simply forgotten. But for me, could never be forgotten.

Maureen O'Sullivan
Inishfree Writers

Plum

Out of the blue
This fine, late summer's eve
Wild, ripe fruit
Has fallen like manna
Voluptuously
On the soft ground
Of my bed
Making the room orchard.
Vapours of
Spiced melon
Sparkling peach
A hint of pepper
Vanilla,
Trace of musk
Swirls in a
Swooning head
And I
Lone harvester
Climbing the
Apples and pears.

Royce Harper
Newtownabbey Writers' Group

Coming to my senses in a *roundabout* kind of way

*O*riginating from a country where roundabouts are every few yards and traffic lights have been part of daily life since 1926, along with ever-increasing congestion, collisions and mounting road rage, it came as quite a surprise to me to listen in on a radio programme that was apparently being taken up by an extensive discussion on 'roundabouts'! Despite the fact that the entire county of Donegal has only one roundabout to its name, it was causing a bit of commotion amongst the road users in downtown Letterkenny.

What, to me, was a subject not worth considering had the inhabitants of Donegal up in arms. Callers were positively irate about the roundabout in question. Some suggested that extra tuition should be taken in order to learn how to negotiate the object of their fury.

I was flabbergasted. All this fuss about a roundabout!

Cwmbran, one of my home towns, built after the Second World War, was awash with the offending items. Roundabouts have been springing up at every junction in Wales from the 1950s onwards and there seemed to be no stopping them. When the Coldra roundabout in Newport, South Wales, was constructed about 20 years ago it was deemed to be the largest in Europe.

And there was me thinking that those postcards depicting two donkeys on a road with the caption under it — 'Rush hour in Ireland' — a cliche of times gone by. Now, according to the radio these donkeys may well, in the near future, be photographed attempting to navigate a circumlocution in the middle of a busy town centre.

However, it wasn't until a few days later when I found myself sitting in the car at the end of my road with the indicator flashing impatiently to the right as I waited for what seemed to me to be a steady flow of cars to pass before I could pull out, that I commented to my husband on the amount of traffic there was on the road this morning. I had in fact counted three cars, when reality struck.

'Donal', I said, 'can you believe I am actually complaining about three cars being heavy traffic?'

After living in congestion-free Donegal for the past eight years I wasn't sure if I wanted a roundabout in it or traffic lights or anything else for that matter that brings stress and overcrowding to these bumpy but peaceful roads.

Well, maybe just the odd patch of tarmac.

Maureen O'Sullivan
Inishfree Writers

Letter

The street-aviary's evensong filters fleetingly, sweetly through
Dinner's on a slow heat. Ray's not due
'Til later... whenever that is?
All the little chores, that frankly take up too much of life
Can damn well wait
I'm at my desk. Music scores piled high, tenuously secured
With ornament, instrument and paperweight
Amassed from far-flung travels, but you know all that
I thought I'd write
While the ambience is conducive
And I'm finishing off last night's bottle of wine, lest it go flat!
It's been too long since I heard from you
What gives?
Surprisingly (perhaps!) the warbling of little birds
Put me in mind of you
Their voice so much bigger than themselves
Shrill, bubbling-brook trills that wash so thrillingly over.
The pregnant pause... diminishing echo.
Not for money or bread do they sing
At crack of dawn, and in the afterglow

I'm holding a picture of you, the costume-party, remember
You came as Sydney Greenstreet, in *Night-boat to Cairo*
Vocal inflections perfected, fez
White dinner jacket, Turkish cigarettes
Only your cummerbund straining
Your middle as wide as my grin
No one could accuse your wit as being so much padding.
Between courses, we sang, 'Will - I - am, William,
It was really something'
I suggested, quite seriously, (though still laughing!)
That you should get an Arts Council grant
Simply to attend soirées,
but I very much doubt if they do that!

All's quiet here
I'm sure it's not the same with you
Do you stride down Piccadilly, an outrageous lily in your hand
Have you drunk the Guinness brewery dry
In that foreign, anglo-saxon land
And stagger, with unmuddy feet to early coffee-stands?
The last wisps of the day are trailing away
Round a dancer's whirling feet (pirouetting to the wings)
And I am sad, though it will pass,
That you could not stay
Life moves on...
You reminded me so much of it!

Royce Harper
Newtownabbey Writers' Group

Womb

Sounds deep seep through my every being
Vibrating
Remembering
Suspended in a womb of orange light
Not unlike the sun's intenseness behind closed eyes
A space to live and grow
Explore and play
The water warm
Teases against her new skin
Her body responds and curls to its honeyed spread
Exploring this space
With its changing colours
Deep red sleeping
Bright orange wakening
Such a happy place to be
Did she ever have to leave

Going Home

Look up
Into the blue
Beyond
Earth's boundaries
Let your soul on wings fly.
Leave your beautiful body
Resting
Heal on earth's sacred bed
And fly into the blue

Border

There was a time
As a child
I hated you

There was a time
As a teen
I began to move
In between

There was a time
I knew not how
I'd ever bridge this divide
I saw you there
And me still here

Time's moved
Events preordained
My simple idea
Of love and wanting
Has without direction function
Brought us to a junction

Stammer

As a child I stood mute
Words bore no flight
Or beauty sweet
But splattered spluttered stammered from
A silent month
Struggling form

In hopelessness impatience
You looked on

Pretending teenager
Flung the words
Cannoned words
Charged
Barricaded
Body Loaded

Today I read my poem fair
In Inishfree not a care
My children's faces in delight
Family neighbours in beauty light
For me my words are not ink alone
But music from my guttural throne

Sister

Fragile broken wounds
Weep for you to look
Completely
See the tears
Hear the bleeding
In loving strokes
Absorb the Leaning
Love this while
Undistracted eyes
Your smile balms
In deepest healing

Unemployed

I was born to create
I did procreate
Now I recreate the garden

I wanted to conduct an orchestra in dance
Now I sign on Wednesdays in a trance
I smile and live a life in gay
At times I struggle with dismay

Round and round and round I go
Where no one knows
Funny thing; I don't think
Living life on a roundabout

Take direction
Don't despair
Everything leads somewhere
Wish tae hell I know where
How to get there

Remember

Noise noise noise
Noise we are
Perpetuating humans
Moving in distraction

Then, for a moment
Like stone in quiet
Motionless symmetry we stay
Like the stone upon your resting place

While dancing dandelion seeds
On an unseen current
Lift and drop
Around us
Between us

We look to the earth
And the horizon
For a future that is ours

Unspoken Words

I seethe and shudder
Your every space terrifies and abhors
tentacles cling and manipulate
Infecting, distorting.
You stand large and loom
Into every cavity invisible unknown.
Your patterns warped and sore
Your cries I cannot bare
For you touch and I shudder
Leave my space
Take your chaos and deceit
Far away
And find a place to
Be calm and at peace

Maureen Browne
Inishfree Writers

Whiskey Priest

A Buzz Lee Adventure

*H*eedless of the broken glass on the oil-streaked tarmac, I went down on one knee and fingered Father Cobner's neck. I was looking for a pulse. Nope. Not that I had expected any.

I had to hand it to the pious old bastard — he sure had a way of making a dramatic exit.

Father Octavian Cobner lay face down, his head wrapped in his arms, one leg curled up to his chest, the other sprawled full-length. The sort of pose used by a corpse in a foxhole or a shell crater in no-man's-land. Or should that be no-God's-land? I don't suppose it really mattered.

He still had his old Webley pistol clutched in his left hand. The hand that shook so badly that I'd asked him once if it was Alzheimer's. He may have been just an old whiskey priest, but goddamit, he was *my* whiskey priest.

I tore away his soiled clerical collar and slipped my hand down over his heart. His body was cold. He'd been dead for a few hours — here, in this lonely spot in Cheshire, a field with a strip of tarmac and a hunk of concrete *circa* World War II.

Father Octavian Cobner. 'S got a ring to it. He'd been a missionary in Africa, South America and the Far East. He had been fluent in Spanish, Portuguese and Malay. It seemed an even worse waste than usual.

He had several layers of clothing on under his clerical black, and even through these I could feel a hard oblong. I tugged at it in its bindings and came away with a book. My first feeling was that it was a Bible, but nope. A small quarto book of poems by Algernon Charles Swinburne. With notes in the margins written in Latin. Wrapped around the small quarto to give it bulk and weight were more than a dozen bullets.

I eased the Webley out of his stiff fingers and broke it open. From the smell it had been fired recently. I emptied out the spent casings and tried six of the bullets. They fitted like Kismet.

The dawn was breaking, cold and grey, an inhospitable turning of a world that was wearing out its own ozone layer. I looked about instinctively for watchers, but the only movement was that caused by the wind: litter blowing across the tarmac; spare, leafless trees performing arthritic calisthenics.

I stood up and noticed that the heel of one of his boots was caked in red paint. Glancing back the way he might have come, I could see half-dried crescents of the paint marking out his progress.

Reluctantly, I followed the line of red heel-prints. The more I saw of them, the splodgier they got, until they showed up as most of the footprint. It was like a schematic of the phases of the moon: from red crescent, to gibbous, to full. I bent and examined the paint. It was something like red lead, used for sealing a car chassis.

The light was increasing about me. Overhead the clouds swarmed in a millrace, dull-grey against a lighter grey of higher, slower-moving impassive cloud. I had nothing better to do today than to find out why an old street priest, an old gutter dweller, had died. His gun had been no use to him, so why bring it with me? Because it was there.

The tracks led me to a cleft in the earth. To call it a cave would be to lend it an unwarranted glamour. I would never have seen it apart from the tracks. A rusted tin of paint had been left to rot there, and somehow Father Cobner had spilt it over his shoe.

I opened the book and flicked through the pages. Copperplate handwriting, elegant and mysterious. The language was impenetrable. My Latin extended as far as *id est* and *et cetera*, but even I could hazard a guess at one of the phrases my eye lit on:

Horridas nostrae mentis purga tenebras was on a page opposite the long poem entitled *The Garden of Proserpine*.

Horridas was something to do with 'horrid' or 'horrible'; *nostrae* was probably 'ours' as in Paternoster or Our Father; *mentis* was something to do with the mentalities or the mind; *purga* was related to 'purge'; *tenebras* was similar to the English word tenebrous or shadow / darkness. So, put that all together and you get something [scratch head, and move lips] like: our horrible minds need purged of darkness.

This line was on its own page in the book; the rest of it was more of the delicate copperplate, with the occasional *hic*, *haec* and half a *hoc* decipherable among the rest of the jumble. Further on were diagrams, smudged with thumb marks, of sigils arranged in circles, with pentangles between and diagrams of candles at the point of each star.

There was another poem entitled *Hymn to Proserpine*. A line from it caught my eye:

Thou hast conquered, O pale Galilean.

Beyond these rather unsettling little doodles were more diagrams that showed the making of the bullets. I checked the tip of one of the bullets and found a cross engraved in it.

'Holy dum-dums,' I murmured. 'But they still didn't stop him from catching a coronary.'

I wondered how long it would be before the body might be discovered. Was there someone whom he might have wanted to contact? If I was planning on getting involved in this, then it would be necessary to do something to protect myself.

'You're a prophet in the wilderness,' Father Cobner told me when I first met him. We were warming ourselves beside heating vents down an alley in the centre of Chester. It's a picturesque city, Chester.

'You're only saying that because I shared my sandwich with you.'

'Not true!' he expostulated. 'I know your face. I've seen you in my dreams.'

'Yeah, yeah.' I turned away derisively, thinking of going somewhere quieter.

'You're Buzz Lee — that American who's wanted by the police!'

That sort of stopped me in my tracks. 'Hey, come on, now. Don't shout out a thing like that or we'll both be somewhere a lot warmer than this, except it comes equipped with bright lights and all the night-stick you can eat.'

Cobner smiled slyly to see my discomfort. 'Never worry, Brother Lee. I can see you have been ordained. You are on the side of the angels. I know, for I too am a man of the cloth.'

He showed me his Bible wrapped in a rosary as if this was incontrovertible proof of his being the Archbishop of Canterbury's right-hand man. I looked at him. I mean really looked at him. I spent a good two minutes looking at him: his fleshy nose, his stubble, his twisted teeth behind his pendulous lips, his thin hair scraped over a narrow pate. He stank. I knew I wasn't too salubrious myself, but he smelt as if he had rolled recently in fresh kaka.

Finally I sighed, releasing the breath I'd been holding unconsciously. 'Okay. So how come you know who I am?'

He pulled out his Webley, and I took several hasty steps backward. 'Right. I get it. You shoot me and then yourself. I go to hell and you go to join the choir invisible.'

'No, no, no.' The gun wagged limply in his hand. 'We have been brought here to the same destiny. I am ready to pass on. You can take my mission.'

His voice was plummy under the slur of red wine; his eyes rodent-bright and feverish. I found it hard to visualise him in a clean surplice and in a church filled with sunlight and stained-glass windows. He looked like a bookie's runner gone genetically wrong. He also scared me, and it wasn't just the gun.

I was looking at my future self. He couldn't have been any more than fifty and yet he was destroyed. The street had decommissioned him. His own demons — or maybe he thought of them as angels — had taken him and sandblasted away the pipe and slippers humanity in him and left a ragged Old Testament scarecrow in his place. Turnip head and a robin redbreast for a beating heart. This was Wurzel Gummidge with his fire and brimstone psychosis head on. All we needed was the burning bush and tablets of stone and we could have had an old time religious experience on our hands.

I cleared my throat. 'Your mission?'

'Yes. The oaks of Mamre.'

'Ri-ight… The oaks of Mammary.'

'No, you don't understand. They are the trees of the covenant. The oaks of Mamre. M - A - M - R - E.'

'M - A - M - R - E. Right, now I get it.'

'They grow in the darkness now,' he said.

'How can trees grow in darkness?'

'Because they have grown *down* into the darkness. *Down into the darkness.*'

'Is that a problem?'

'They will bear fruit in the darkness. They will drop their seeds in the shadows. A forest will spring up. A dark forest.'

'Mirkwood?' I suggested.

'Come again?' he said, his turn to be nonplussed.

'Forget it. It would take too long to explain.'

But he took his time explaining it to me. Not all at once. And not on the first night we met. But eventually it got explained. It didn't make much sense, but it got explained. The oaks of Mamre; the trees of the covenant. Genesis 18:1. The place where Abraham was visited by the LORD. Pretty famous Bible story. Three men (angels, actually) appeared to him at these trees. He sent for his missus to wash their feet and set themselves awhile under the shade of the trees. The three angels of the LORD were on walkabout to check out the nightlife in Sodom and

Gomorrah.

Before that, Abraham built himself an altar to the LORD there. It was the place where Abraham went the day after Sodom and Gomorrah were destroyed — he had a grandstand view of the smoking valley where the cities had been. That's the region where Abraham and his wife, Sarah, were finally laid to rest.

Why is all this important? Beats the hell out of me. But it meant a lot to old Father Cobner. The trees of the covenant. He mumbled the phrase to himself like a mantra, gumming it over as if it was a sort of spiritual cud.

I would see him occasionally then miss him for a few days and he would show me something in his hands: a leaf that had been torn to resemble a profile of Christ. He carried a green switch with him once and flagellated himself with it through his clothing as he walked the walls of Chester. Then he broke it and showed me the sappy inside, bubbling with resin and juices.

'Behold,' he said, 'I break the branch and Christ is within.'

An old Gnostic saying, that.

He tossed the stick into a litter bin and passed on. Then, as if an afterthought had occurred to him, he returned to the litter bin for a rummage through its contents. I hadn't sunk quite as low as that, but the possibility was always there. Life on the street was eroding my sense of disgust.

We had been around a few corners, old Father Cobner and I. If we had been Holmes and Watson, we could have lived together in 221b Baker Street and had a plump Mrs Wosname bring up her home baked goodies on the hour every hour. We had adventures. Isn't that an old-fashioned word? We had 'em together. There was an inextricable, inexplicable chemistry working between us. Like the effect of Algernon Swinburne's verse on T.S. Eliot, his company drugged me and over-whelmed. I could escape him, but we always met up again. Neither seeking the other, but finding, always finding. When the moment was opportune; and when it wasn't, that too pleased.

A little soul for a little bears up this corpse which is man.

He had saved my hide a couple of times and I had pulled him out of a few sticky situations. So, where had I been when he had copped this? Why hadn't I been here, too?

I remember the way we parted,
The day and the hour we met...

And here I was, I had to go down into that cold, dank hole. *In a hole in the ground there lived a hobbit. Not a nasty wet hole…* Yep, this one was nasty, wet and dark. If it was short and brutish too, then I could hack that. I've hacked a hell of a lot worse and come gibbering through.

I thrust the Webley into my overcoat pocket and jammed the book next to my heart, binding it about with my various layers of tank-tops, liberty bodices and string vests. Then I lay down and stuck my head into something that I was making my own business. I was just hoping that it wasn't a hornets' nest.

Even as I crawled through, the name Proserpine popped into my head. I remembered who she was. She was the Roman version of the Greek myth of Persephone, who was stolen by Hades (who was a guy and not just a place) and taken down to the Underworld. Persephone is the Queen of Hell, but originally she was called Korè. She was brought to the Underworld but her mother mourned for her so strongly that Zeus directed that she should only spend three months of the year in the Underworld. This has been taken to symbolize the growth of seed-corn in the earth. It is buried for three months and when it sprouts, its golden colour is the sun fallen to earth. Picturesque, these ancient religions.

Growth in the darkness. The oaks of Mamre, growing in the darkness. What sort of sad, psycho-sexual mess did Father Cobner have festering at the bottom of his libido? I was afraid I was going to find out.

The hole in the earth was very close and made several sharp loops. I couldn't truly crawl, but was capable only of corkscrewing my way through. The rebirth ramifications of this ritualistic act were not escaping me when I felt my head enter a more open area underground. I struggled through and lay for a moment in the darkness to catch my breath and steady my nerves.

The darkness was absolute. Even after some few minutes, no light from above the ground leaked down through the tunnel. I always carried matches nowadays, so I pulled a few out and struck one. The sharp smell of sulphur as it kindled made me sneeze.

The light revealed a cavern the size and rough shape of a railway carriage. I had probably crawled down about thirty feet, and the roof was about ten feet overhead. Rubbish underfoot and the vintage of some of the food wrappings showed that somebody or other had used this place over the last twenty years. The place was dry and rustled underfoot with bundles of dried flowers. Bouquets brought to this dark shrine had been laid here to desiccate. A mummified corpse of a big dog lay to one side. A sad reject Kerberus, whose bark had been much worse than his bite. The body had a collar on it with a name tag. As my first match flamed out, I could just read the name: Fido. *Fido* — I trust. I always thought it was a dumb name for a dog until I learned it was a Latin title. Then it made really deep sense. Fido — I trust. But what had he been entrusted with?

Were these the flowers of Proserpine's garden? Was this Cobner's own personal Underworld? And, if so, what had he fired his pistol at?

I struck another match and found a packet of candles. I lit half a dozen and placed them in wax-raddled niches in the rock walls. As the light grew about me, I could see that there were images drawn directly onto the walls. They were simplistic but powerful figures, drawn in a matchstick style, but numinous with their content. They showed antlered figures, half-men half-wolves. Plants and trees depicted through a child's eye of a green landscape, grey jagged sierra mountains, a sky as simplistically blue as the real one, a sun in gold spray paint; Halley's comet borrowed from the Bayeux tapestry; a rainbow arc of sunlight and beyond it was the dark night, picked out with spangled stars, planets with improbable rings — and beyond them lay the Powers and Principalities. These figures were still stick figures, but they had grown or evolved to produce figures that were formed from labyrinthine windings. The spray can had started at a point and meandered until a devil or angel had been conjured out of the dark rock. And the continuous line had woven them all into a tapestry of torment, a hieratic frieze of one man's personal theogony.

I lit all the candles and placed them in their customary niches. And still there was a darkness at the far end of the cavern. I took one of the candles and carried it forward into the darkness, my feet turning on the accumulation of rubbish. Each step produced a clank or a rustle or a hiss as I pressed on the last puff of an aerosol can. Then, underfoot, the rubbish just seemed to end and I was walking on bare limestone rock.

The walls were farther away than before so that the candle afforded me only a globe of light that bobbed in a sea of darkness. I had become disembodied, reduced to a pair of hands in the candlelight, the scuff of boots on the rock.

Then I stumbled. The candle went spinning out of my hands and the light blinked out. I knelt down to retrieve it, barking my shins on an unseen outcrop. My fingers skittered over the rocks ahead of me — then paused.

I could feel roots ahead of me. Gnarled tangles of tree roots. They were immovable, but how they could grow out of the seeming living rock I couldn't tell. Despite myself, my fingers gave up the quest for the missing candle and followed the roots forward into the darkness. The tubers broadened and grew round and buttress-like, snaking up and back into the rock. The roots joined and formed a trunk, a broad bole of knotted bark with ridges broad enough for a man's finger to slide into. Even in the darkness the tree bark exuded a sense of history. They weren't just old, they seemed to shed oldness, bequeathing antiquity to those who came in contact with them.

Somehow — although it doesn't make much sense when I recall it — the cave was forgotten. The fact that it was dark was resolved in my mind because I told myself it was night. You don't have to be underground to find darkness, right?

The bark of the tree invited me to climb. It would have been a sin to refuse such an invitation. It was as if this tree had grown here specifically for this moment, like a subterranean redwood that had been a mere sapling when Christ had climbed his own particular suffering-tree. This was Yggdrasil, Odin's world-ash. This was the centre of a universe — not just any universe — but *my* universe. A very compact and bijou universe.

So I climbed. My fingers followed the tactile labyrinth they traced in the darkness and soon my face encountered the first of the branches and dew-laden leaves. The cool splash of liquid on my forehead and eyes was like a baptism.

I found my first fruits and nuts, all growing on the same twig. Apples and hazelnuts. Apples for folly and hazelnuts for wisdom. I could smell the faint, ethereal perfume of pomegranates from somewhere ahead and their rinds threatened to burst under the weight of succulent flesh. I picked an apple and brought it to my lips. I inhaled its subtle scent, rubbed the waxy skin on my upper lip, broke the skin with a tooth and the flesh underneath was white. Even in that darkness, the colours blazed through as *gnosis* after *gnosis* came home to me.

My ears were filled with the crunch of my working jaws as I chewed, the pop and whine of sinews inside my skin deafening me to the song that was being sung somewhere below the tree. I knew the song had been going on for sometime — the way you know such things. You realise it has been there, encroaching on your attention.

There was a girl singing somewhere below. A soft, lilting refrain that told me all about her. The song was her. She was the song.

The darkness was lightening, like a scene on a stage with the lights coming up and several layers of scrim fading away to reveal the action. I knew that the place was an orchard, and the grey walls beyond belonged to a religious college. The girl was dressed in the grey pinafore of a novice. She had her dark hair filled with apple blossom, like stars melted into a tropic night. She had a guitar, and she was singing with a smile on her face and in her voice.

A man lay at her feet, toying with the fallen apple blossom. And he was Cobner as a young man. And when the girl stopped singing, she put aside her guitar and they kissed. And the kiss melted them back into the darkness, back into the animal champing of my jaws. I might have been a dormouse that the Romans had introduced to fatten up for a banquet — and with as much sense of history.

Underneath my hands, the bark of the tree groaned. The crevices that had served as such kindly handholds broke open and revealed that they had teeth. The tree was rocking like a runaway tramcar and trying to eat me alive, to consume me as I had just consumed a little part of it.

The apple of folly... now, why couldn't I have broken the cycle?

With a tearing screech, I felt a huge mouth crack open just under one knee. The teeth were short and molar-like, ready to grind me down. Canines are for cats, but trees like to take their time with you. Molars will do nicely, sir; all the better to grind you with.

The tree rocked and I was up to my waist now inside the crack-like mouth. I could feel a deep throat with my heels, the sap dripping like mucus over my thighs. Then I remembered the old Webley. Is this what Father Cobner had fired at? Is this what had reached out for him? — out of the darkness — to squeeze his heart like a sponge. To pop open his coronary like a nut in a vice?

There was a horrendous gobbling sound going on down below. The tree was slavering, thicker and faster. My clothes were soaked with the sap that frothed and fumed about its maw. I spread my legs to try to avoid slipping down the gullet and reached into my clothes for the gun.

The first shot went off by accident. I felt the heat of the blast through my clothes, the way my hand bucked with the force of the recoil. The tree suddenly stopped moving. And this new silence was deafening, this new stillness was worse than a frenzy of death throes. There was such an air of studied tension, of deliberate poise, like watching an opponent and waiting to strike at his weakest moment to catch him off-guard.

I fired again.

The tree rocked to its roots with a shudder that felt like a world dying.

I fired again.

It felt like another nail in my own coffin. I wasn't freeing myself from anything by this course of action. The tree had been a liberator, it had promised to show me the Knowledge of Good and Evil, my eyes would be opened and I would be *like a god, knowing Good and -*

I fired once more.

Eeeeeeeee-villlllllllllllll. The sap dried on my skin and puckered my pores into goose-bumps. The tree rooted into my head, its roots were the axons in my central nervous system, its branches were the bulbs in my skull I fondly called my brain.

I fired again.

For a tree to grow to heaven, its roots must reach to hell. I felt as if my spine was being torn out from my ribs. A fisherman had slid a knife into my pelvis and gutted me. Now I was filleted and the fish-knife was slipping cleanly through my ribs. I was spread out like a herring and tossed in flour. *Though your sins be red as scarlet, yet I shall wash them as pure as snow.*

I fired again.

Loveliest of trees the cherry now is hung with bloom along the bough. I think that I shall never see a billboard lovely as a tree. Bent every twig with it, every branch big with it. When men were all asleep the snow came flying... Flying, flying flying, O Lord thou pluckest me forth, flying.

I fired again...

... and the hammer fell dully on a spent cartridge.

My brain felt clogged with mud. My mouth was filled with acrid tasting pulp. My fingers were clasped about the butt of Father Cobner's Webley. Talk about your actual Ovid's *Metamorphoses.* I felt that I was Daphne, turned to a laurel. A dozen other mythological characters all turned into trees — everything from Narcissus to Minthe.

My head was clotted with blood. I sat up, moving stiffly, and felt dried blood crack on the skin on my face. The cavern moved around me. The candles had burned down to mere nubbins of wax, their light little more than sparks about to plunge into their own personal heat-deaths.

Envoi

Who, what, why, where and when?

I couldn't answer then and I can't answer now. I knew I had the claustrophobic tunnel back into the outside world, the uterus from one abyss to another. Panic welled up in me at the thought of being in such a rocky, unfriendly throat. I don't know how I did it, but I got out. The gun was lost and it was the afternoon outside, and the body of Father Cobner still lay there where I had found it.

It would be nice to say that I brought him back down into his own personal temple, his *temenos* dedicated to whatever gods may be. But

I couldn't face that darkness again. Instead, I waited until nightfall and carried him to a nearby road. There I hitched a lift to Chester where I stole a car.

The car I used to ferry Father Cobner to his own Isle of Avalon. I'd had enough of gloomy Hellenic Underworlds, what we needed was a sprightly Celtic Island of the Blessed, a Tir naN-Og where he and his apple girl can linger over their music together.

He's buried on an island in a boating lake in some amusement park. There I know he will enjoy the frolics of childish moments, and there the only apples are covered in candy and the only nuts are ready salted, shorn of any wisdom.

Jim Johnston
Newtownabbey Writers' Group

the pitfalls of being a poet!

i'll take my pencil

for a stroll down

by the tide's edge

look for my favourite rocks

one looks like a giant frog

sit in my magical cave

think of all my loved ones

in far away places

noisy streets full of cars

people and shops

forget the night

stumble back

across the island

no torch no moon

or stars to show

me the way home

but the luminous sand

my pencil worn

down to a stub

the pitfalls of being a poet!

it's taken flight

skylark or swallow
caught in the conservatory
could not tell the difference
it happened so quickly
   had left the door open
      for it to escape
   my white cat surprised me
      crept in and clamped
         the poor bird
      i managed to rescue it
origami bird legs like sticks
   so fragile walked up the garden path
      hand gently out stretched
         its eyes bright as a new penny
            looks me straight in the eye
               and before i know what next
               it's taken flight!

hitch hike

hitch hike
along the shore
road nobody stops
too many cars
going too fast
round twisty bends
a black van
stops just as
i reach the seaweed factory
holidaymakers maps everywhere!

july or walking on sunshine

life is a rage of melodies
i try to grasp the tiger's tail
as it disappears
into a blue
hearted shape
of a hole
in a brilliant sky
full of white cloud banks
that slowly move through
a windy afternoon
one blade of grass
gets caught in a cobweb
hanging from the window frame
dancing up and down
a conductor's baton
for a symphony of scenery
blue denim washed sky
busy deep blue green
sea of white froth
bushes dancing to and fro
to one's inner music
july or walking on sunshine

trees of mystery

on our tiny island

there is hardly a tree

just lots of granite

heather bits of bog wood

one lonely hollow

with trees bent

in one direction

blasted by the salty

winds off the atlantic

no cloud forest

buttress roots

of a cedar mangrove

black juniper

king billy pine and bunyan tree

just the wind looking for trees

anyone for toast?

sometimes

you have to think

about answers

you want long enough

then they somehow

pop up without warning

like toast anyone for toast?

i try

i try

and count

the rain drops

on the window pane

lose count

most of them

stay in one place

half a dozen or so

run all the way

down to the bottom

of the window pane some don't

barry edgar pilcher
inishfree writers

Planning Ahead

𝒫eter sat with fury so much a part of his expression as he recalled the past. When he first obtained the post of cashier in the large bank in the City, he was ambitious and full of self confidence. Consequently he applied himself to the job with total commitment. Now fifteen years later he was known as the chief-cashier. He didn't earn the prefix 'chief' by merit, it mockingly indicated he was the longest serving cashier in the bank. Peter's path to promotion had long ago crumbled under the tread of the manager's relatives.

There had been several opportunities for promotion. On each occasion when Peter wasn't chosen for the post he was given reasons by the Manager.

'I need a good reliable man at the grass roots to deal with trivia... That's the foundation of any good business... Couldn't cope without you... A valued member of staff... Trustworthy.'

Peter knew it off by heart. He had developed his own natural immunity to the patronising compliments. On previous occasions he had replied at intervals in a monotone voice, 'Yes, sir... Thank you, sir... I understand Sir,' as he fixed his gaze at the manager's slogan on the desk: *Plan Ahead*. But on this occasion he was determined not to be tossed about like the small change in the bank. He waited until the manager had finished speaking, and then he said, 'I am better qualified for the post. I do not agree that your nephew...' As he was speaking he realised he was being dismissed by the wave of a hand, and in that dying moment his reservoir of self-esteem drained dry.

Unlike the manager, Peter was a very popular member of staff. He always put the welfare of others before his own. He had infinite patience with new members of staff and was always willing to help anyone coping with a backlog of work. But now he did not hear the genuine sympathetic murmurs of commiseration from his colleagues as he sat in a turmoil of humiliation and bitterness. It was the words 'to deal with trivia' which disturbed Peter most. After fifteen years' dedicated service, was that the measure of his worth... to deal with trivia?

Peter stared at the slogan on the wall and swore softly. The cursed thing was everywhere. *Plan Ahead*. It was then Peter decided to do just that.

A priority in the bank was the security of valuables and cash. After 3.30 p.m. as clients and members of staff left, the door automatically closed behind them. A strong-room in the basement was used solely for the storage of cash. It operated on a time-lock system, being impenetrable between the hours from 5 p.m. until 9 a.m. weekdays, and from 5 p.m. Friday until 9 a.m. Monday. The only members of staff who held a key for access to this strong-room were the manager and the chief-cashier.

The cashiers balanced their receipts daily, then handed the cash to Peter who collated the figures, drew up the balance sheet, and then placed the cash in the strong room. At 4.45 p.m. precisely, the manager would enter the office for Peter to accompany him to the strong room, where he would cast a practised eye over the balance sheet and the bank notes stacked in neat bundles of £5,000 and £10,000. The manager believed it was necessary to stand beside Peter and confirm the strong-room door was properly locked. There were a number of occasions when he had actually stood listening for the sound of the time-locking mechanism clicking into operation at 5 p.m. The whole process was conducted with monotonous regularity.

There were now delicate differences in Peter's habits. He started to carry a small travel bag to work. Some days he would go out at lunch time to do his shopping, on others he would leave the office at various times in the company of members of staff and then say goodbye when they reached the supermarket. He also tested his ability in the strong-room; to calculate how many bundles of notes he could pack into a bag in two minutes and five minutes. But most of all, Peter took a fascinating interest in what happened on Fridays.

He noted that Friday night's holdings were well above the average £500,000, and he knew the reasons why. Friday was also a popular day for staff to leave early; even the manager would enter the office four minutes earlier than usual to do the cash check. Nothing trivial about that! Peter had noted everything about everybody over a number of months now. He even knew the time of the flights to South America between 5.00 and 7.00 p.m. on a Friday. The only thing left to do now was wait for Friday.

On Friday Peter went out at lunch time with his shopping bag, but the only purchase he made was a one-way ticket to South America.

The cashiers gave him their receipts and cash at 2.00p.m. There was notification of two large amounts for withdrawal at 9.15 on Monday morning, and at 3.15 p.m. there was a large amount of cash lodged. All exactly as Peter had anticipated. He drew up the balance sheet and placed the cash in the strong-room.

The manager entered the office at 4.41 p.m. precisely! He and Peter went to the basement where the manager carried out the cash check, giving the usual condescending nod of approval as Peter locked the strong-room door. Then he headed off home as Peter returned to the office.

It was 5.20 p.m. when the last of his colleagues wished Peter a good week-end before leaving. Peter cleared his desk, put on his jacket and carried his shopping bag to the strong-room. Unlocking the door, he stepped inside, closing the door behind him. He stood for a few moments savouring an explosion of pleasure. He could visualise with clarity the manager's face on Monday when he would open the strong-room door and realise he didn't *Plan Ahead* for this event.

Peter packed all the cash into his bag. It was 5.40 p.m. when he locked the strong-room door for the last time. He experienced a pang of regret that he had been unable to say goodbye to those he had worked with for years. Yet strangely, he had a much stronger feeling that deep within them, his colleagues would be pleased that his ability would now be widely recognised. Aboard the plane to South America Peter left behind all thought of the trivial tasks he had been responsible for over the past fifteen years. One of which was resetting the time mechanism on the Friday of the Spring week-end when the clocks went forward one hour.

Sarah Barrett
Newtownabbey Writers' Group

Black Joe

My Special Little Friend

𝒯hank you for the innocent, simple and unforgettably happy times we shared in Inishfree.

Black Joe, his wife Teresa and four children, Martin, Paul, Joseph and Lisa, now reside in Wales.

These are some of my memories of him as a little boy on Inishfree.

He was just eight and a half years old when I came to live on Inishfree in June, 1963. A handsome boy, gentle, sensitive, full of fun and mischief, with a mop of thick black hair, and an unbiddable tuft at the front which refused to lie down. Immediately, there was a meeting of spirits between us and we became inseparable friends. Often that first year we went hand-in-hand. It was the most natural thing in the world for us to do. The following year or so he had outgrown that stage, but secretly, I feel we both treasure that innocent time.

Each day after school, I would look forward to see

From left to right: Black Joe, Helen McCann, Eddie Ned, Barbara McCann. The McCann family were regular visitors to Inishfree at that time. The donkey was named Tom.

him hurrying past Charlie-the-Hill's, over the fields clutching his schoolbag, wave to me, rush up home, have tea, and in no time at all reappear, running past Winnie's* and Eddie Ned's to join me in whatever I was doing. If I were working at the turf, hay, or painting the boat, I would make sure he knew where to find me.

Perfection!

One sunny day I put blankets to soak in the bath. There being no electricity on Inishfree, I couldn't have a washing machine, or such like conveniences. I could have hot water, though, from the gas boiler.

Meanwhile, the sea was inviting, so answering the call, Black Joe and I changed into our swim suits, and joined by Tootsie and Toby (the cats), and our loveable big elkhound Finn ran, in high spirits, to the beach just a few yards from the house.

Jumping off Moonrock was one of our favourite sports (Finn's too), and the tide today was just,

PERFECTION!

Carrying Tootsie and Toby over the deep water and setting them on the rock (they insisted on being part of everything), we would jump off, swim around (seeing who would get there first) to the far end, run over the rock (the cats joined in this bit), and repeated it over and over again, until exhausted and exhilarated. After some sessions of this, we felt marvellously refreshed, invigorated and ready to tackle the blankets.

But first things first. After shaking themselves thoroughly, and something to eat and drink, the animals stretched contentedly on the grass, allowing the hot sun to dry them out. From their favourite vantage place, the rise in the lawn, outside the big bay window, they could watch all proceedings inside the house and outside as well.

Now it was time for our welcome cup of tea, and a slice of Winnie's delicious homemade bread, baked just that morning in the pot-oven over the open fire, with red hot coals of turf on the lid. When ready, (how she gauged it I do not know, you can't see through an iron pot!) it was lifted off the hook and placed on the floor. Then came the tricky part; lifting the lid evenly and steadily without spilling the spent coals, ashes and soot all aver the bread, floor or yourself. Winnie, with the tongs, gripped the little centre handle of the lid, and with the experience and knowledge of her seventy years, performed all this hot, heavy work with ease and great panache. The pot tilted to the side, and the

---

* *Winnie was my mother-in-law. Mary Kate, her neice; Eddie Ned and Eddie Hugh Tony, my neighbour.*

bread caught in a clean tea towel. There it was, deep, the full size of the pot, the rich tantalizing smell filling the kitchen, the thought of a thick slice with homemade butter melting on it making the mouth water.

She used to enjoy the expression on my face. I could only marvel. No matter how often I watched her, she never failed to amaze me. Most important of all, she was great fun and always welcoming, her warmth and spontaneity filling the kitchen. Like a magnet, all were drawn and wanted to stay.

Winnie was expert, and no bread baked in any other fashion could come up to her standard. Never in a hundred years could I bake bread like her. She didn't weigh the ingredients, just (seemingly) with carefree abandon, threw them together in the basin, and the results invariably and inevitably

PERFECTION!

But perhaps it was Winnie's own happy generous make-up that was embodied in her baking, giving it the wholesome lightness.

Now well fortified, and bursting with confidence, we felt ready to challenge any washing machine. With salt water, clean feet, and a lot of stumbling and laughing, we took turns treading up and down the bath on the blankets. When it was Black Joe's time, I kept feeding him chocolates — just to keep the wheels in motion! With fun like that, who wanted a washing machine?

Between us we managed to carry, or rather trail the basin outside and spread the heavy wet blankets on the rocks. The results when dry,

PERFECTION!

Precocious Calves and Precious Linen

Dirty laundry now presented no problems. With our washing procedure worked out to a fine art, Black Joe and I — considering ourselves 'quite expert' — agreed that on the first perfect sunny day, we would launder the precious linen.

One day while helping Winnie to spring clean, she showed me a large brown paper parcel tied with string. Taking it from the handmade wooden cupboard, she carefully laid it on the bed.

'We don't have many worldly goods but what's in this parcel is precious.' With family pride in her bearing, she undid the string.

I gasped in appreciation — each item was exquisite — table and altar cloths, big and small, pillowcases, bed linen edged with delicate hand crotchet — all heirlooms going back generations, each with its own memory of the past and the people who created such beauty. I was

Close friends
Eddie Hugh
Tony's donkey,
Foley, and Finn.

conscious of the privilege of sharing this special moment.

The linen, with age and long storage had become slightly soiled, especially at the folds and I offered to launder with extreme care.

Now the perfect washing day had come. Up Black Joe and I went to Winnie's for the parcel. Mary Kate, with a kettle of boiling water, was outside on the green, scalding the churn. Winnie and she always did the churning together, and preparations were in full swing. The sunshine affected our spirits and after some lively banter we left with the linen.

It was hard work, as extreme care was essential, but after some hours, we stood in the back garden and surveyed our work. We had every right to feel pleased and proud. On the long line stretching across the garden, pristine white, hung the precious linen and three 'best' white shirts of Patsy's — all dazzling white in the sunlight.

In about half an hour's time some would be ready for ironing. In readiness, I got out the ironing board and the gas iron. Needing a short break we decided to tell Winnie and Mary Kate our good news and also give a hand with the churning.

Eager to resume and finish our very important work, within the half hour, we hurried to the back garden and stopped dead in our tracks. It was worse than any nightmare. All along the bottom of the washing was a bright grass green ragged edge. Irreplacable crotchet, lace and linen, the arms and tails of Patsy's shirts all eaten away, and at the very end of the line two little calves happily chewing the last item on the line!

In an hysterical frenzy Black Joe made a dive for the calves — their little innocent faces registering surprise at the sudden fuss. 'Get out, you wee divils, out, out, out, God Almighty what a mess!' In a state of terrible shock, I collapsed on the back steps, my head in my hands and wept. 'Oh my God, how am I going to tell Winnie?'

The calves safely back in our neighbour Eddie Hugh Tony's garden, we sat on the steps together.

Choking with emotion, our eyes followed the bright green line of destruction, and the desecration of the precious linen.

'Winnie is good — she'll understand,' Black Joe softly whispered, trying to comfort me.

And he was right. Although sorrowful, Winnie's philosophical nature, sense of humour, her understanding and love for animals (especially little calves) came to the fore. Eddie Hugh Tony was also upset when he witnessed the disaster. But Winnie said 'It isn't the end of the world. It can't be helped' and did her best to ease our misery.

And on special occasions when Patsy wore his 'best' white shirts, we all laughed when he was unable to remove his jacket — there was either an arm or a tail missing!

Margaret Duffy
Inishfree Writers

Tanka I

Above a giant body of sea
Lone gannet sets its sights
An airborne David
The white missile stabs

Tanka II

White, needle-fingered froth
Biting the lip of a wave
Pulling it in a daze of senselessness
To a happy death on the shore

Tanka III

Heart stirs in fitful sleep
Head hears its subterranean moans
Eye spies what the flesh desires
Conscience muddies the pool
With clumsy feet

Tanka IV

Swallow streaks by, slash of black, white
Bee's squiggly-line bobbing
Sparrows hop. The eye darts
To every tiny summer skirmish
Encore: silently clapping butterfly wings

Progress

From once lush fields
Skirting Carnmoney Hill
The cry of the corncrake
Is no longer heard.

Pause

Such dark eyes
Big as a baby's
Unsettling momentarily
As I undid the buttons
Of her blouse.

Delicate

Breeze from the open window
Shaking the bay tree leaves
My life on a thread
Will fall as one of these.

Royce Harper
Newtownabbey Writers' Group

Danny

There are many sad stories connected with Arranmore Island, and one of them concerned my own people in 1907. It was the month of June and the weather was beautiful. Jimmy Grainne Rodgers, my great grandfather, was off to Burtonport for the day, but left instructions for all the jobs that were to be completed before he returned. The eldest sons, Paddy and Jimmy, were busy threshing corn on a slab near the house, so the father told the middle boys, Mickie, Jimmy and Frank to finish their tasks around the little farm before taking the large brown cow up to the pasture on the mountain. The youngest boy, Danny, who was eleven years of age wanted to join the others. However, Jimmy Grainne said no, he was too young, and must stay round the house to be of any help to his mother or his sisters, Kate and Grace. He could draw water from the well or keep the fire going with the turf while the women baked and prepared meals. Danny was not pleased. The morning passed until it was time for the brothers to set off for the mountain, and Danny pleaded with his mother to let him accompany them. Eventually, Jimmy Beag, the second eldest brother assured the mother the boy could come to no harm — what danger or problem could there be with three older boys to look out for him.

The boys enjoyed their afternoon up on the pasture. As the cow grazed, they lay in the heather talking about school, their friends, their oldest brother Paddy's recent marriage to the priest's housekeeper. Then cheery shouts rang out and they were joined by two of their friends who had brought a battered old ball. They tossed and kicked it around for another hour until the cow's lowing reminded them it was time to be off home. The cow had been tethered with a long thick rope, so Mickie untied it preparing to go. Danny wanted the job of leading the cow down, never having done it before. He shouted and jumped around Mickie who at last agreed and wound the thick rope round and round Danny's thin shoulder and upper arm. Just as they turned down the passageway, there was a loud clap of thunder. The boys had not noticed the change in weather and all eyes turned skywards. The poor cow, however, taking fright at this loud noise began to gallop down the passageway. Danny ran, trying to keep up, but the impetus of the cow's dash was too much for the little boy. He lost his footing and being attached to the cow with the rope still round his arm, he was dragged for many yards. His little head and body were battered on the rocks, and only when he became wedged between two large boulders, did the cow slow down, then stop. The other, rushing and slipping behind, sobbed and cried as they looked down at the little body huddled by the rocks. Mickie unwound the last of the rope, while the others ran to the nearest house for help. Men came running with blankets and tenderly carried the broken little boy to Greene's house. The priest and doctor were sent for but no-one could help — Danny had been battered to death on the rocks.

When Jimmy Grainne returned from Burtonport, he was told the awful news and brought to Greene's house. Beside himself with grief, he walked from room to room carrying the pitiful little body still wrapped in blankets. For hours he would not part with the child, until his broken hearted wife, Kate, pleaded with him to bring their child down home to be prepared for burial. The whole island grieved over the loss of little Danny.

The family's grief was partly assuaged five months later when the wife of the oldest son, Paddy, gave birth to their first child. He was a healthy baby boy who was given the name of Danny — named for the dead boy. This baby was to be my father.

A Childhood War Memory

*a*s a child during the Second World War life was quite exciting and of course we did not appreciate the worry and sorrow affecting the adults — that is, until it touched one's own family. My mother's brother James, a dark handsome youth of nineteen, joined the Navy. As a five-year-old niece I was so proud of this sailor in our family, and looked forward to his short leaves home. He would bring laughter and life into Granny's house, and toss me into the air with lots of kisses and cuddles. I could not understand why the adults cried saying goodbye to him on his last leave — this was a new turn. Of course I did not know that his training was over, and he was sailing away to combat in the seas off North Africa. That New Year, everyone seemed subdued — missing James' company, and all talking of war news. With my cousins I listened to snatches of adult conversations. We children used to sit under Granny's dining room table, listening and giggling, at some rendition of *The Last Rose of Summer* or *It's Twelve and a Tanner a Bottle.* To hear now any of the songs that the aunts and uncles sang then, transports me back instantly to those family gatherings in Granny's, and the warmth and security we children felt sitting under that table with a plate of Aunt Mary's rock buns to eat.

Then at the beginning of 1941 the war brought great sorrow to the family. It was one week after James' twentieth birthday. I was at school when the teacher called my name to go over to the Master's office. To cross from Infant's school to Mr Curran the Master's room was an exciting adventure for a five year old. Why did he want to see me — I was a good child! When I entered his room. a big girl, Teresa Grant, who lived in my street, was standing beside his desk.

'Teresa will take you home, Kathleen,' he said.

I did not ask him why — but once Teresa buttoned my coat on and we started up the road, I wanted her to tell me why I was being sent home.

'I've not to tell you,' she replied. 'So, stop asking me, and walk faster.'

A few neighbours were standing on the street outside Granny's, but stood back to let Teresa and I go in the gateway. When Teresa opened the door my mother appeared, pulled me into the bathroom and locked the door. What could be wrong to make my mother cry the way she did and hold me so tightly to her I could hardly breathe? I still remember the fear as I thought 'my Daddy is hurt in the pit.' Then my mother told me 'be a good girl when you go into the living room to see Granny', she could hardly speak for sobbing. 'Uncle James has been killed in the war and gone to Heaven.'

I was more curious than sad — I'd never personally known anyone who'd gone to heaven — did he go in his ship or did the angels carry him in their arms? Was he shot or blown up? I didn't ask my mother, of course, as she took me by the hand through to Granny's living room. Why were the blinds drawn in daylight? I thought. And why were all these old ladies sitting there with my Granny?

My mother left me standing awestruck by the big armchair inside the living room as she went to answer the front door. No one noticed me as I quietly crept under the table. I sat there for hours listening to the fresh outbursts of weeping as each visitor called to offer their condolences. Fancy the priest and old Dr. Scott visiting Granny at the same time! I don't remember my Granny making a fuss, but as each member of her family arrived all the other old ladies would begin lamenting again. My daddy came home early from work, and I heard them discussing how to get word to my grandfather who was working in England. When my cousins arrived they joined me under the table, and although we were affected by the atmosphere in the house, it was more because we found it hard to cope with our parent's grief, rather than we were sad for poor Uncle James.

'After all,' we said to each other, 'fancy our uncle away to see Jesus, Mary and Joseph. Will he take his uniform off and put on a long white gown? Will he get his dinner there, and why did no one remember to give us a meal?'

Although out of sight under the table I knew when my Granny Rodgers arrived. My heart lifted as I heard her soft Donegal voice, and whatever words she said, my Granny Martin at last broke down and cried. The sorrow in that room seemed to us children like a physical weight pressing down and creeping under the table to smother us.

Next day I found to my delight I was quite a celebrity at school. Apparently, after I had been sent home the day before, the Master sent a note all round the classes giving the news of James Martin's death. He was the first young man in our parish to die in the war, and of course the Master and all the teachers knew him well. I felt quite grateful to Uncle James for creating this interesting situation at school — big boys and girls who'd never before spoken to me, crowded round at playtime and were kind to me.

When the memorial cards for James arrived a few weeks later I thought the puzzle was solved as to how he'd gone to Paradise. The cards showed a sailor lying stricken on a ship's deck with Jesus standing stretching one hand out to him. The verse read, 'Greater love than this no man hath, than a man lay down his life for his friends.' How wonderful! I remember thinking. It was Jesus Himself who came and took Uncle James by the hand to Heaven. Our family should stop grieving.

For Lena

From the little island chapel on a grey and wintry morn,
The mourners silent came, together and apart.
The prayers and simple sermon from the visiting priest with
Holy Mass had surely touched each heart.

They walked in silence to the little graveyard,
Along the cemetery road by Chapel Strand.
All full of grief for Eddie losing Lena.
Great Atlantic gently lapping on the rocks and sand.

The priest had told us how she loved God's creatures.
She never worried others with her cares.
Could we bring comfort to her bereft husband?
We joined in with those final words and prayers.

Then suddenly above the intonations,
A lark began to sing with springtime joy.
Oh heaven-sent bird to uplift with your warbling,
Our hearts so sad, depressing thoughts destroy.

We know that God has taken Lena to Him.
Her years of ill-health o'er, and tho' she's gone,
Our faith was strengthened — Then the lark fell silent,
His little task for God and Lena done.

The Turf Cutter

We watched him stooping over as he toiled up the brae,
An old man with hair and swinging arms.
His steady gait soon took him o'er the mountain on his way
To the peat bogs just beyond the last two farms.

Later that day we walked this road to view the cliffs and sea,
And on our way we passed him footing turf.
'A fine day for your walk,' he called. 'I think I'll take a break,
I have a flask of water, will you join me for some tea?'

As we sat there in the peat bog, he told us wondrous tales,
Of Fionn MacCool, Cuchulain, Oisin and Deirdre too.
His lilting voice transported us o'er Rosses' hills and vales,
Happy listeners almost hypnotised by sparkling eyes of blue.

We turned to wave but he was busy cutting with his spade,
Such grace in every movement as he bent and threw out sods.
Brown sinewy arms and pliant back, his legs like steely rods,
No old man this, quite ageless, toiling there in lonely bogs.

We saw him coming home again, swinging down the brae,
Jaunty battered straw hat set upon the back of his white head.
'T'was grand weather for the turf,' he called, 'but to end a
    perfect day,
A pint of Guinness and a song, then I'll be off to bed.'

The Wake on Gola Island in 1952

There's been a terrible tragedy we were told in Arranmore
Young Michael McGinley and a Scots girl found dead upon the shore
On Gola Island to the north, they were trapped under the curragh.
'We must go to wake the dead,' said Jack the Glen.

'You know his sisters well,' said Jack, 'you too must come along.'
Such a sad sail north that aftenoon, no whistle or a song.
I remember Philly steering and the silent boat of men,
'It is good to wake the dead,' said Jack the Glen.

As the little isle came into sight an eerie sound was heard
It seemed to float across the waves like strange calls of a sea bird.
I turned in alarm to look around at the ululating sound.
'They are keening for the dead,' said Jack the Glen.

Before the house of mourning was a long, low, whitewashed wall
There the grieving island women sat, each wrapped in her black shawl.
As our boat was tied up at the slip, the wailing rose and fell.
'God help them in their grief,' said Jack the Glen.

The McGinley sisters greeted us, their friends from Arranmore
They cried out and they hugged us as we stepped across the floor.
Chairs were pulled around the fire, tea and drinks were poored for
    those
Who had come to wake the dead with Jack the Glen.

I can ne'er forget the scenes I saw that summer afternoon,
Or the sight of their dead brother laid out in the upper room.
Such a young dark, handsome man in brown scapular and shroud.
'Let us all kneel doon and pray,' said Jack the Glen.

'Why did he have to go, he was all we had!' they cried.
But only God knows why such a fine young man had died.
We hoped our prayers would help them, but our hearts were oh so sad,
As we walked back from the wake with Jack the Glen.

That little Gola island is deserted now, no one's home.
I oft see it from the plane when to Donegal I roam,
But still there is the low, white-wall where the keening women sat
When I went to wake the dead with Jack the Glen.

Kathleen Rodgers Brady
Inishfree Writers

Black and White

(The cattle raids)

It began, he said,
A long, long time ago;
The Opé stole our cattle,
And they should know
We will not settle
Until they're gone.
Hear the word of the Karamajong.

It began, he said,
A long long time ago;
They stole our cattle
And they should know
We will not settle
From the time of *Táin*:
Sunday, Friday
Bleeds on and on.

Drumcree

I put to my blind father
The rough skin of an animal
So he knows not who I am,
And blesses me, the brother,
With all the land.

And again
Sometime,
I walked a road in Ireland,
Where my brother held the way,
and his father
threw a hand to shore
and blood ran
through the bay.

So,
I must come to know each hand
And the footstep when it comes,
Hear them speak a sweeter word,
Hear no chosen tongue,
So I can sleep in comfort
With the final whisper done.

Ephron's Field

This is nothing between us,
A field, all its borders
And a cave for Sarah.

But it will be for silver, he said,
Gave four hundred pieces
And laid her down.

And when it came to his own time
the words again came round,

This is nothing between us;
Abraham,
Sarah,
Ephron the Hittite,
The field with all its borders,
And the cave.

Now they squabble over Hebron;
Trenches multiply like stars;
Four hundred times four hundred,
Each death empowers no wish to yield.
Can they not recall
A stranger gave a stranger
Hebron's field.

Now the grass would cover up the stone
And the stone would give the grass no bed;

Perhaps if Ephron's oxen still could tread
A furrow to be sowed,
Through Hebron's streets
Through Dunloy,
Up Garvaghy road.

The *Sea Empress*

After Braer
The *Sea Empress* lay off Copeland
And swam the Farset
To be healed, converted for her sins
By the warm congregation of the war.

And all the filth she spread
Along the coast of Wales will be forgiven,
Will be gone, whilst
The soiled hands of churchmen
Struggle on.

Dublin to Belfast

The certainty
of the train.

The biblical next.

No falling off
keeping to the text.

Time
tread
undone by the telling
of the town on fire,
where we must get down
at Portadown and walk,
give up the tear to foreigners
who came to see the peace
but got Drumcree,
and the blistered hands and feet
of history.

Stones

Amongst all of them
you could find yourself
swinging in a sling
making the hard kiss
upon the forehead of the giant.

In the hands of a convert
build a temple wall:

A rock before the tomb
being the heaviest door of all:

Reigning down on each new word
or the path that goes abroad.

Jeremiah 6

And the Book falls open here.
Evil appeareth from the north
And great destruction.

It was
seven
nine eight.

Dread the Hill
Ditch, barricade:
See crusades of unmade graves
Faith so keen to turn a spade.
See hands push through waves of fire
To hymns that can reach no higher,
From a voice unsure of freedom or prison wire.
Which colour drapes the truth, the liar?
But red the children in the fire
And black the spire.

I Used to Live Here

I used to live here
Opposite the peeler
Who snipped and sold his flowers,
Beside the nurse who polished
Hound and sea horse
On the Minor parked outside the door:
Shiny hubs and lamps that blinked
Our lady of calomine and zinc.

To think I played against the rails
Of the big red school
That was opened for the daft
But rarely put a foot upon the path,
Even then I felt that fortune
Wasn't all that far away:
St Catherine's wheel had not so much
As touched a single hair.
My Sunday school attendance card
Marked up with care,
Wheel and pew, still and hard.

These were the homes of the almost poor
Who beat the way from North Queen Street
To have grass below their feet
And knew what schools were for.
How to make Fortwilliam they must have thought,
Then the wondering dream fire caught.

O God what a day when I told P6
That I wouldn't go to work in Gallaher's
Or the Yard.
It would be ether, plaster, blade.
They all stared.

But they were all nice people.
McKnight's mobile store
Two doors away,
Mister Garret's white straw hat
Then we got television
And watched England with the cricket bat.

This is where people owned the street
And kneeled to keep it clean,
Where last evening
They tortured several motor cars, beat them,
Fired with oil
As if to make all armies coil
With handkerchiefs aloft
And now they're wading in the road;
Soft, black boils to let.
Why is it easier to forget
Great ships on walls of ice
Than the auld mistake
That comes back twice and thrice;
Almost as often as it likes.

I used to live here
Where Mr Crozier worked in a pin-striped suit,
Where my friend made ballet shoes of glass,
Where we watched the Russian sputnik pass
And followed it to the sea like some Canute.

The Spirit of Drumcree

The spirit of Drumcree
Spirit
Holy spirit
Holy ghost
Ghost
Gone
And the spirit free.

Stephen Potts
Newtownabbey Writers' Group

Bilder

Die Urgewalten dert Natur
  auch in mir.
Vernichtende Stürme in mir
  tobend.
Zerreißende Blitze mich
  durchfahrend.
Tosende Wellen durch mich.
Peitschender Regen wie
  Tränen?
Sonnenlicht! erweckt zu
  neuem Leben,
Sonnenlicht durchflutet mich,

Bis der nächste Sturm
Die jungen Triebe der
  Hoffnung bricht.

Immerwährendes auf und
  nieder
Zerstörend-Emeuemd?
Doch mit der Zeit sieht man

Das was wahr ist
bleibt!

Images

The elemental powers of nature
  also in me.
Destroying tempests raging in
  me.
Flashing of lightnings passing
  through me.
Roaring waves through me.
Lashing rain like tears?

But light of sun! revives to new
  life.
Light of sun flowing through
  me,
until the next storm breaks
the fragile beginnings of hope?

neverending up and down
  destroying?
renewing?
But within the course of time
  you may see
that, what is true
  remains!

Heidi Schulz
Inishfree Writers

The Tenant

Narrow stairways, lightless,
huddled drunkards, sightless
tenement halls, peeling walls,
noisy strangers, foreign calls.
Friendless ...

Grimy windows, blind-less,
junkie children, mindless
damp and rot, spit and snot
smell of mould, growing old.
Decaying ...

Landing floorboards creaking,
rusting doorlock squeaking
seventh floor, unpainted door,
turn key slowly, fingers sore.
Open ...

Dark and dismal, cheerless,
rodents watching, fearless
close the door, seventh floor,
switch the light on, blessed poor.
Welcome ...

Dripping walls, paper peeling,
feeble bulb, yellowed ceiling
yellow light, impending night,
search for pince nez, fading sight.
Fumbling ...

Dampened walls, dripping,
blow on fingers, nipping
haw of breath, cold as death,
empty fireplace, coal bereft.
Lifeless …

Fingers painful, biting,
matches, fumbling, lighting
hissing gas, heat at last,
soup-filled saucepan, poor repast.
Hunger …

Ancient sofa, leaking hair,
toe-less slippers, threadbare
mufflered throat, overcoat,
shawl on shoulders, eyes remote
Freezing …

Fading light, winter night,
getting colder, no respite
painful standing, shuffling tread,
gloomy bedroom, truckle bed.
Sleepless …

Surging memories, better days,
mother cuddles, toddler plays
schoolboy fancies, summer dance,
stolen kisses, first romance.
Love …

Young man, working, meagre wage,
independence, come of age
strong and handsome, black of hair,
full to bursting, free of care.
Youth …

Formal greeting, coyly glance,
secret meeting, soft romance
fondness growing, special thing,
planning, vowing, golden ring.
Wedding …

Fumbling, learning, settling down,
doctor, smiling, belly round
Midwife, pacing, next of kin,
bawling, toothless, silken skin.
Daughter ...

Years of laughter, golden,
thanking God, beholden
endless days, tender ways,
gentle hours, scent of flowers.
Contentment ...

Countries quarrel, needless,
warning, threaten, heedless
leaders blether, armies gather,
country needs you, husband, father.
War!

Mud and trenches, lying,
wounded, dead, dying
putrid smell, crashing shell,
legions falling, earthly hell.
Bedlam!

Rushing headlong, firing,
comrades fall, expiring
flashing bayonet, slaughtered foe,
foxhole taken, on we go.
Hero!

Homeward coming, cheering,
home in ruins, fearing
family missing, lack of news,
stand and join the breadline queues.
Homeless ...

Job to job, lifeless,
daughter missing, wifeless
bitter tears, passing years,
clouded future, never clears.
Hopeless ...

Eighty years, nearly,
missing family, dearly
dismal bed, nodding head,
grey eyes drooping, prayers said.
Sighing ...

Sinking, slowly falling,
'Daddy!' someone calling
radiant light, dispels the night,
wife and daughter, shining white
running to him, heavenly sight,
arms around them, grasping tight
laughing, joyous, soaring flight.
Dying ...

Seventh floor, unpainted door
old man sleeping, evermore
cold and hunger in the past
painless, smiling, peace at last
Heaven!

Gerry McAuley
Newtownabbey Writers' Group

Don't Believe Everything You Read

In 1497 the Italian born explorer John Cabot sailed from Bristol in his ship the *Matthew* and discovered Newfoundland. In 1996 in Bristol a replica of the *Matthew* was launched. In 1997 the *Matthew* sailed from Bristol to Newfoundland as part of the Cabot 500 celebrations.

In January 1996 in Bristol, Daniel O'Donnell attended a charity afternoon to help to raise funds for the rebuilding of St Patrick's Catholic church. The event which was organised by an Irish lady called Amelia Dunford was well attended and a grand afternoon was had by all. Afterwards many people approached Amelia with the suggestion that a club for Daniel fans to get together could be formed in Bristol. Amelia contacted as many Daniel fans as she could and arranged a meeting. The meeting was successful and very productive. It was decided to call the club 'Daniel's Friends South West England', and that we would meet once a month on a Sunday afternoon at St Patrick's church hall. A committee was elected and Amelia was asked to act as chairperson. Of course all of this had to be reported to Ritz and their approval gained.

I was a member of the committee and at one of the early meetings I suggested that as Daniel's Friends had been launched in Bristol in 1996, as had the *Matthew* — would it not be a good idea if we joined in the Cabot 500 celebrations? The idea was accepted and Amelia asked me to take the project on board (excuse the pun).

I wrote to the letters page of the Bristol *Evening Post* saying that Daniel's Friends South West England, a newly formed society for fans of Daniel O'Donnell were taking part in the Cabot 500 celebrations and would like to form friendships through correspondence with the people of Newfoundland. Would any readers who had friends or relations in Newfoundland please contact us? Also if anyone would like to join Daniel's Friends, they would be most welcome.

A few days later I received a telephone call from a reporter on the *Evening Post*. She said they had received my letter and would like to make an article out of it. I said fine, it would be publicity for Daniel and for our club. She asked all sorts of questions and then asked me to arrange a get-together of the committee for photographs. A little later she rang back and said that they had changed their minds about photographing the comittee. They wanted to send a photographer that afternoon (Saturday) to take photographs of Colin and me outside our house, and also to the Colston Hall where Daniel was in concert that evening to take photographs of us with Daniel. Fine, no problem. On the Monday although I had retired the previous week I went to work so that my assistant who had been promoted into my job could attend college. I had agreed to work for just one week so that she could take her exams. On the Monday lunch time I went to the newsagent to get a copy of the *Evening Post* to see if they had printed the promised article.

Shock, horror!

On the counter there was a pile of *Evening Posts* and there on the front page was a picture of Colin and me with Daniel and an article about this couple who had sold their bungalow to retire to Ireland to live next door to Daniel O'Donnell. No mention of Daniel's Friends or Cabot 500. We hadn't sold our bungalow at all, we planned to move in February to the Dungloe area for three months to see how we liked it. We most certainly did not want to live in Kincasslagh and especially not next door to Daniel O'Donnell.

The rest of the week was hilarious, most of the English and Irish papers took up the story. Sky TV sent a team to the house to interview us and so did ITV. We appeared on the TV all over the UK including Northern Ireland as well as in the Republic. We were interviewed over the phone by Radio Bristol, RTE, BBC Belfast, Radio Ulster, Radio Leeds, Radio Kerry, Talk Radio London, North West Radio Donegal etc. Most of the radio interviews were done while I was in the office so it was a good job that I had an understanding boss. Christine Lewis, the reporter who started it all off rang to make her peace. I told her it was okay except that she hadn't printed anything about our club. She promised to rectify that, and true to her word she did.

We came to Dungloe last February as planned and decided that we definitely wanted to retire to the area, but not too near to Daniel (can you imagine all those fans popping up day and night? Only joking — I think). We looked at houses but decided that by the time we had paid for repairs and alterations it would be cheaper to buy a piece of land and have a house built. We eventually found a suitable site a couple of miles out of Dungloe just off the road to Kincasslagh. We had plans drawn up, applied for and received planning permission. Then and only then did we put our bungalow in Bristol on the market. We put it into the hands of an estate agent at the beginning of October and in one week he had a buyer who was happy to pay the asking price. How lucky can you get? We completed and moved out on 26 November 1997, just a year after the *Evening Post* printed the article about us.

Our new house is being built by a local builder and is due for completion in the middle of June. We are at present renting a furnished cottage just across the road from our site. We are here until the end of May, the cottage will then be needed for holiday lets. Luckily we have a motor-home and we will spend the last couple of weeks in it. By that time we should be able to park on the site and hook up to the electric and water. It will be a relief to get our furniture and other possessions out of storage, especially all my Daniel memorabilia.

Stephanie Handley
Inishfree Writers

The Cormorant

(Corvus marinus)

Low over the waves
Of the lough
The black dart slices
Darker than shadow

Alights on a jagged pole
A wrecking distance
From the pebble-heavy shore

Tall, and thin
As a tarred stick
In a sharp, sea-breeze
A solitary sentinel
Surveys the alien sands

Then the unfolding
Of great, sleek wings
Showing the imprisoned night —
Day.

Royce Harper
Newtownabbey Writers' Group

A Postman's Lot

*E*arly in my Post Office career I was given charge of an electrically-powered parcel delivery vehicle. It was similar in shape to the 'Prairie Schooner' of Wild West fame. When I pushed the handle into the down position my covered wagon charged forward at the breathtaking speed of three miles per hour.

Among the other paraphernalia of Post Office officialdom I was introduced to was the Recorded Delivery book. This innocuous looking little yellow-coloured book caused no end of problems for us postmen. Anything entered in it had to be signed for by the addressee, and if after three attempts to deliver the item concerned had proved unsuccessful, it meant more form-filling for the postman involved. Parcels, packages and letters were usually easy to deliver, but on occasions there would be letters from the Lord Chancellor's office — usually threatening court proceedings — or summonses from the County Courts. Getting people to sign for these could prove very difficult.

Imagine then my feelings when on the second or third day of using my parcel trolley I was given the dreaded yellow book and warned to watch out for a package. I was about halfway through my round when I came upon the item concerned. It was a very securely wrapped package measuring approximately six inches by nine inches, and all the corners were heavily sellotaped.

When I knocked on the door it was opened by a lady whom I judged to be in her late fifties. Putting on what I hoped was a very cheerful expression I said, 'Good morning love, I have a package that needs signing for.'

I was astonished when tears began to roll down her face. Without saying a word, she signed the book, took the package and closed the door.

When I returned to the post office I related to an experienced postman what had seemed to be a very strange incident. When I had finished my story he looked at me with a very condescending expression and said, 'Did nobody tell thi lad, 'er 'usband deed last week? That were 'is ashes tha were delivering.'

Ramblings of a Rural Postman

*I*t was a dank and foggy morning in November and I was telling myself that there must be easier ways of earning a crust than by lugging 'Her Majesty's Mail' around.

I had just completed the steep climb from the main road and was trudging through the churchyard behind St Mary-le-Ghyll church. My silent mutterings were suddenly interrupted by a thin, croaky voice that drifted out from an open grave. "What time is it mate?'

I froze for what seemed an eternity, but could only have been a few seconds! I ceased to function as a thinking human being. As the ice thawed from my spine I very slowly turned to face the open grave. From this yawning gap, and equally slowly, there emerged the head of our local gravedigger.

With a nonchalance Sir Lawrence Olivier would have been proud to display I glanced at my watch and replied, 'It's a quarter past ten.'

He looked down into the depths of the grave and said, 'Come on, lad, it's time for a pot of tea and a sandwich.'

He and his apprentice then scrambled out of the half-dug grave and disappeared into the relative warmth of the coach-house for their morning break.

I am sure I completed my round with a much springier step than I had when I started it.

John Threlfall
Inishfree Writers

Fortune's Favourites

$\mathcal{I}$t began with an ache, a hunger, and it would not let her be. She looked out over the drab, smoke-enveloped English suburb and her heart sank. A bedraggled sparrow pecked at the soot-encrusted windowsill. Down below she could just make out the outline of the occasional ornamental tree, the half-dead shrubs. There was a meanness about the landscape. It was a monochrome collage of factories and houses and pocket-handkerchief gardens. At night the shunting of the trains kept her awake. Clare never got used to it and she never called it home.

To while away the long night hours she recalled another time, another place and the lush greenness that was Ballyhone. It was a mistake to think of it because it made the homesickness worse.

She should have known, for hadn't Biddy McCracken told her it would be so. Biddy who had never ventured more than a few miles from her own cottage and couldn't possibly have known what homesickness was. But Biddy was a bit of a witch, or so people said, the best fortune-teller in the county.

To reach Biddy's small farm you had to negotiate a long dark lane, a fierce dog, a cat that was frankly manic and Biddy's son Michael Joseph, who though he had never been known to do anyone any harm was strangely menacing in his own quiet way.

Biddy would tell your fortune just once, for, she said, they came from all arts and parts, at all times of the day and night, and she was scundered with them. She never took money, because she acknowledged hers was a rare gift, but she did accept the odd present of tea, or sugar, or 'a few wee buns for your tea, Mrs.'

Biddy was gifted. She would never give bad news like a death or serious illness. She just wrapped such things up in such a parcel of obscurity that people gathered there was something amiss and that they should be careful. The 'tall dark strangers' and the weddings and the births predicted always came true and naturally people were always eager to return. They tried to disguise themselves with wigs and scarves and spectacles, but Biddy never forgot a face and she would send them away with a flea in their ear.

The one exception was her neighbour Clare McMeekin whom Biddy said was like a daughter to her. Clare was welcome any time because she did not abuse the privilige. With Clare she shared the gifts when there was a glut. It was Clare who trudged over the fields with Biddy's pension and groceries, who called to see if they were all right when snow or floods made roads impassable. Clare tended them the year they both went down with flu and it was she who drove Micky to the hospital when he had one of his funny turns and collected him again when he was better.

Yes Clare was more than welcome and Biddy would even point out to her the symbols in the teacup — the bells for a wedding or celebration, the cradles for a birth, the tall straight leaves for a man, the shorter leaves for a woman. Again, she would point out the pictures in the fire and she'd laugh her cackly laugh, stroke her downy chin, look over her half-moon glasses and say to Clare 'You'll soon be as good as me at the fortune telling. Sure I'm training you to take over so I am.' Clare would protest vehemently, a shiver would run down her spine, but Biddy would pat her hand, smile her enigmatic smile and say soothingly. 'There, there, I know you wouldn't want that. I realise that you will have your own ambitions, but I would just love in my heart if you were here for Micky when I'm not. You're so good with him. He likes you. 'But don't you worry now,' for she read the look on Clare's face. 'I know it can never be and I'm content so I am. Really I am.'

Anyway, the last time Clare sat in Biddy's kitchen she had been nursing a large cup of tea and a scratch on the back of her hand. Biddy's cat Morph did not share Biddy's fondness for Clare and frequently spat at her or scratched her when she tried to make friends with it. Sometimes Clare wondered why she kept on visiting the McCrackens but Biddy was such good company. True she was a bit odd, but she had a fund of good stories, she enjoyed a good joke and she produced the most intricate crochet work which Clare was eager to learn. At Clare's home beyond the fields there was just her mother and father and her four younger brothers. Clare loved them dearly but had to admit they were not noted for their stimulating conversation or ready wit.

Biddy handed Clare some homemade herbal salve for her hand, took her empty cup and peered inside.

Her face took on a petulant look. 'This pain is nothing to the pain you'll know hereafter when you try to live in a foreign city,' she warned cryptically.

Clare eyed Biddy warily. In vain she protested that she had no intention of going anywhere. Micky had crept in the door silently and settled himself in his usual chair. Both eyed Clare with hurt expressions.

'It's in the leaves,' said Biddy.

'She read it in the leaves. She's never been known to be wrong,' echoed Micky.

'It will not let you go you know,' admonished Biddy. 'There's something in the fields and rocks and trees that will pull you back. This land has always known how to draw back those whose minds are finely tuned to its call.'

Clare again protested her innocence. It was no good. Biddy peered and sighed and stirred the fire and sighed again. And within six months Clare found herself in the soulless suburb that was Wembley, with a job she could have liked and people she could have warmed to if the invisible cords would only stop pulling at her.

Clare had been the eldest in her family and when her father died suddenly she had cut short her studies and started looking for a job. The Civil Service was the first post that became available but they could not offer her a job in Northern Ireland. They could and did offer her an attractive post in London with a generous salary. And so Clare became the breadwinner and the only time her soul sang was when she posted the monthly money order back to her mother.

When she had been in London about a year her mother wrote to inform her of Biddy's death. Apparently Biddy had known for some time that she was seriously ill but never said anything. Clare was saddened, but with a new and exciting man in her life she had little time to dwell on it beyond wondering what would become of Micky. Within a month she received another letter from a solicitor in Ballyhone informing her that Biddy had left her the cottage and small farm on condition that she kept an eye on the welfare of her son Micky.

Clare couldn't believe it. Why should Biddy leave her estate to her? Surely it should have gone to Michael Joseph, her only kin.

'But from what you've told me he's a bit of an imbecile,' said John, her fiancé. 'That will be the reason. He's non-compos-mentis, not capable of managing his own affairs.'

'No, he's not mad exactly,' said Clare. 'He's just a little bit strange and very, very quiet. He's quite nice really.'

'Well, you go home, my love, bung the half-wit in a home, sell the farm and come back to me soon,' said her fiancé.

Clare looked at him. She was beginning to feel uneasy about the whole situation and she couldn't think why. Yes, she would go home and sell the farm. She would try to arrange a really nice home or some sort of sheltered accommodation for Micky. She would make sure he was really happy before she went back and she would keep in constant touch with him.

A fortnight later she sat in Biddy's chair, in Biddy's kitchen and surveyed her inheritance. Biddy's spirit permeated the place. Her books, her shawl, her slippers, and her crochet work were all in the usual place beside her chair. There was no sign of Micky. People said he had gone missing after the funeral. Clare was worried about him but she fancied he wasn't far away. A bright fire burned in the grate. A bunch of wild flowers in a cracked vase sat on the table as if to welcome her and she imagined she could smell his pipe smoke.

A cold draught blew in. Clare shivered and drew up to the fire. But she still couldn't warm up so on a sudden impulse she draped Biddy's shawl around her shoulders. There, that was better, but her feet were still cold. Biddy's slippers looked warm and inviting, she would just kick off her shoes and slip them on. Yes, they were a perfect fit. Biddy's crochet work was close by. She wondered if she could remember the stitches that Biddy had taught her. She picked up the hook and to her amazement it was easy. Her fingers were agile and deft, she flew over the pattern. But the work was intricate and she was having trouble focusing. She wondered if Biddy's spectacles would... Yes, of course, perfect eyesight now. Bemused she stroked her chin. There was a fine down there that she hadn't noticed before.

Clare stared into the fire and into the future. What she saw there did not alarm her. She smiled and when she looked up Micky sat in his usual chair smiling back at her. The cat Morph jumped up on her knee and purred contentedly and she said to herself. 'I'm content too, so I am, really I am.'

And the next day she posted the ring back to her fiancé.

Margaret Ardill
Newtownabbey Writers' Group

Monumental Peace

(Ulster 1969-98)

There will be memorials, of course,
Cast in copper and in bronze and stone
To these our troubled times,
Now that the blood is drying into history.
Yet, which of these will recompense
      the victims or their heirs?
And who can name the heroes anyway?
Only a clear expanse of starlit sky
      innocent of helicopter's clanking flight,
A dawn bringing new life not threatened by
      the trigger of a gun,
A heart that's free and unafraid
      beating in every breast,
Are what must make effective monument
To what was lost or won.

An Gleann Nar Tógadhmé

A note on translation

In post famine Ireland the Irish language was fast disappearing with the people who had emigrated or died.

The young Douglas Hyde, son of a Protestant Rector in Co Roscommon, who was studying at home due to an illness, realised that something precious and irreplaceable was slipping away. He set out to learn the language himself. So proficient did he become that he later became a major force in the revival of Irish.

It is on record that when Hyde entered Trinity in 1880 he left the intelligentsia dumbfounded by stating that his favourite language was Irish. 'Irish?' exclaimed classical scholar Crook. 'Do you know Irish?' (unthinkable). 'Yes,' said Douglas Hyde, who was to become one of the founders of the Gaelic League and, later still, first President of Ireland, 'I dream in Irish.'

I offer opposite my translation of one of his best loved poems. A beautiful vowel-sounding piece of Irish poetry does not translate easily into English, but hopefully the idiom of today helps to retain something of the rhythm and flow of the original.

The Glen where I was Raised

From place to place I strode about
High jumping I atop the hill;
I was into ships and boats
With joy my beating heart was filled
Like a hare's foot was my own,
Like steel each sinew and joint,
Gladness there was all about
In the glen and I a growing boy.
What cared I for any man,
What cared I for the whole world wide;
I ran as fleet as any deer,
As mountain streamlet running wild.
I could do anything in the world
If only I just wanted to;
The boat skimmed high along the tide
In the glen and I a growing boy.

It isn't that way with me now,
Swift was I who now am slow,
I don't know what it was that broke
Suppleness of limb heart strength of old:
An achiever I, I learnt a lot —
But found in it no lasting joy —
Ah could I but be back again,
Young in the glen, a growing boy!

Anna McCann
Inishfree Writers

Glenarm

Near white, dusty cliffs,
and long pebbled beach,
rooks squabble in lofty nests.
Peat smoke
like incense,
drifts in salty air.
Narrow streets,
of neat little houses
huddle together,
where brown river is king
and the patient heron waits.
There, standing together
like brothers,
old castle wall, and bridge
look out, on a misty sea,
with just, a little church,
between them,
and eternity.

Billy Stewart
Newtownabbey Writers' Group

If you want to write a poem

If you want to write a poem, don't delay.
Get a pen and piece of paper right away.
Don't wait for inspiration for poetry's a craft.
A pot pourri of words and phrases is first draft.

Writing's about bleak pages traversed by moving hand.
Not a finite science, nor ephemeral, nor grand.
Democratic process, deep personal elation.
Because the finished product is your very own creation.

Carefully chosen language in blank verse or in rhyme
Natural and uncontrived, strident or benign.
A universal message, easily understood
Evocative portrayal of atmosphere and mood.

Like a sculptor with a chisel start to hone
Rearranging and selecting and cutting to the bone
Refining to perfection, disposing of excess
At last you are confronted with success! success! success!

Unplanned Meeting

Yesterday I met my love of thirty years ago
Stirred to the depths and shaken by feelings I used to know
Guarded, self-conscious, red hair flecked with grey.
Embarking on a phase of life with children gone away.
We looked and we talked and we searched for a sign
Of how we'd survived the ravages of time.
We talked of regrouped families and folk we used to know
And bitter-sweet remembrances of oh so long ago.

Time shifted back to a carefree youth —
Of mis-spent hours and a quest for truth
Of family politics bringing pressure to bear
Of drifting apart — not seeming to care.
Each memory stabbed me with such pain
Regret replaced blood in every vein.
And yesterday's meeting is plaguing my heart
There is no change — though we're apart.

Retribution

My mother is old-fashioned and she cooks a simple meal.
I'm better educated and there are times when I feel
That courage, imagination and panache could compensate
For dullness — although wholesome — that confronts me on my plate.

One night when everyone was out I put my plan in action
(I had to do it secretly, in case there'd be reaction.)
Conglomeration of ingredients — all mixed up with precision.
A tasty meal would welcome them — result of my decision.

I must admit what I produced was a culinary disaster.
It looked just like the poultice that preceded sticking plaster.
I overturned it on the grass, a stone's throw from the door
Wished it be magicked from the scene — undiscovered evermore.

A lone gull cruising spied me and called out to its kin.
Squawking, squabbling, screeching, they made an awful din.
They 'magicked' in vast numbers and eyed it with suspicion
Wheeling, circling, diving, they kept me in their vision.

In ever-decreasing circles, they approached the wretched meal
Keeping a safe distance from the food they planned to steal.
At last the bravest glided down — all caution to the wind
He dipped his head and strained and gulped — well pleased with his find.

The others swooped down on the place — raucous, noisy, thrusting.
Exquisite movers, plumage smooth, watchful and entrusting.
Consumed with greed and hunger and passion so intense
They gulped, devoured and scavenged those doomed ingredients.

Like vultures round a carcass, they closed in on their prey
Then suddenly, with flap of winds, they rose and flew away.
No tell-tale signs, no trace remained of what had been dinner.
I beamed with joy at my unplanned ploy, an unrepentant sinner.

But sometimes at the dead of nigh, I hear a plaintive yell
A distressed child? A wounded cat? It's very hard to tell.
The seagulls round my mother's house are noisy to excess.
Maybe they'd tone their screeching down if I'd own up and confess.

Shirley Ohlmeyer
Inishfree Writers

Family Ties

*I*t's good to have strong family ties. Just like the Jarlows. They had an awful lot of children who were known for their loyalty to each other. The girls wore each others' clothes and the boys were always seen together. There was a number of mixed marriages among the Jarlows. You know, Catholics and Protestants, that sort of thing. But everyone was treated the same and religion never caused any strife between them. That's just how close they were.

Maggie Murphy lived in the house opposite me, and Peggy Smith lived next door. The Jarlows all had houses further up the street so we knew them well. They would do you a good turn and they never broke the law, just bent it a little. We called them 'rough diamonds'. Not that I noticed any of this myself. I'm known for minding my own business. That's why Maggie and Peggy would tell me things. They knew it wouldn't be repeated.

There were hard times in our community in those days. Many a visit was made to the pawn shop. Mrs Jarlow was known as a 'good manager'. Some said she was so good she could even have pawned the dish cloth. That's probably why she didn't mind at Christmas when all the family piled into her house. It didn't seem to bother old Dan Jarlow either. They called him DJ. There were some people who wondered where they all sat in the two up, two down house. But when family ties are that strong, I believe in live and let live. Oh yes, they were a close family all right, even when they fought.

This happened every Saturday when some of them went down to the pub for the day. Not that I begrudge any hard working man his pint of porter. But once the stout started to take effect, things always went the same way. There would be yarns spun, then good-natured bantering, followed by the fight. The more sober locals knew exactly when to leave the pub. Others, though, seemed to get a cheap thrill out of the Jarlows making a spectacle of themselves.

It was near the twelfth, that Saturday when I saw old DJ and his son-in-law, John, going to the pub. He's married to DJ's daughter, Molly. My Jimmy and Maggie's husband, George, had already left because they always liked a seat near the door.

They were all having a good time, when the singing started. My Jimmy told me the barman doesn't usually allow singing. But apparently the crack was good, and everyone was having a quare laugh. Then DJ started to take a hand out of John.

'Hey, boy!' he said. 'No party songs allowed.'

'What do you mean, party songs?' John said crossly. So DJ started to chance his arm: 'You know fine well what I mean. One of them party songs. I heard you hum it under your breath.'

John got angry then, so he started to sing *The Sash*. That was when old DJ remembered John was a Protestant, so he started to throw senile punches. My Jimmy and George Murphy came home at once. Jimmy told me all about it and said not to go out the door because the Jarlows would be coming up the street fighting.

Well, I was in a predicament. I still hadn't brushed the front, and I always have a clean front on a Sunday morning when people are going to Church. So, fight or no fight, I went out to brush the front. Sure enough, they were coming staggering up the street, arguing and cursing at each other. I could hear DJ threatening to give John a thick lip.

'You and what army!' John said.

I thought it was just as well John's dog came running to meet him at that moment. But suddenly P.C. Brown came down the street. I went into the house immediately as I didn't want to become involved.

Maggie Murphy called over the next day. As soon as I answered the door, she said: 'What was that carry on all about last night? I'd just come out to brush the front, but my George told me to come in at once as we don't get involved in that sort of thing.'

'What sort of thing is that Maggie?'

She pulled down her brows. 'Whatever that carry on was about last night, it seems the Jarlows were causing a rumpus. Not that I heard any of it myself.'

'I know as much about it as you do, Maggie. I'll have to go in. I'm sitting in the middle of my dinner, but I'll see you later.'

Then Peggy Smith called, and she started about the rumpus last night.

'I just happened to have my window open and heard it all,' she said.

'Heard what?' I asked.

'I heard DJ say, "Constable! That dog isn't licensed!"'

'Well, we all know it's a serious offence not to have your dog licensed, even though money's scarce,' I said.

She didn't listen, but went on: 'And John said to the constable, "It is, it is?"'

'That's good,' I replied.

Peggy continued: 'But PC Brown had taken out his little red book and John got a summons.'

'Oh dear, are you sure, Peggy?'

'Yes, positive! They'll not be staggering home together this Saturday, I'll bet,' Peggy went on triumphantly.

'You seem to know more than I do, Peggy. Everybody knows I mind my own business.'

She nodded her head in agreement.

Well, it was no surprise to me when DJ and John walked down the street the following Saturday to the pub. As it happened, I was the only one who'd got the story right.

Because, on the previous Saturday when I saw Constable Brown coming, I distinctly heard DJ say to John: 'I'm going to tell him that bloody dog isn't licensed.'

I went in at once and when I saw our dog was sleeping and quiet, I remembered I had to go up and close the front bedroom window. That's when I saw Maggie Murphy peeping out from behind the curtains in her parlour. She can't mind her own business!

Well, I just couldn't help overhearing the conversation below. I didn't want to close the window immediately as the noise might have made the Constable think I was listening. So I heard the whole thing. DJ did say 'Constable! That dog isn't licensed.'

But John didn't say a word. He was shocked into sobriety. That's when the constable licked his pencil and took out his wee *black* book. But after the Constable went away, John said: 'When I tell my Molly what you've done you'll be in serious trouble. She'll make sure *you* pay the fine, *and* the licence!'

The shock at good drinking money being wasted made DJ sober up as well. Besides, he'd forgotten just how close the family was. So they walked up the rest of the street in silence.

That Peggy one sees everything. My Jimmy says she must sleep on the window ledge. I'd second that, and I find it really annoying, because she never tells anything back properly. As for Maggie Murphy, she hasn't an ounce of sense because she left the hall light on. And the door of her parlour was open while she was peeping through the curtains. Furthermore, I saw her being pulled in from her front door by George, him holding tight to their dog as DJ was shouting, 'Constable! That dog isn't licensed!'

I like the Jarlows. They would do you a good turn.

Sarah Barrett
Newtownabbey Writers' Group

127

The Heron

The sculpted heron stands, patient and petrified
Long limbs sentry-still. Glassy-eyed.
Watching and waiting at strategic spot.
Suddenly he ducks and dives, quick as a shot.

With slap of wings he wheels and flies upstream
Broad now, as tall as he once had been
Extended. Easy rider on the air.
He floats away and I am left to stare.

PLATE I

PLATE 4

PLATE 5

PLATE 16

Bird Commentary

The pheasant is pleasant
He squawks as he walks.

The starling's a darling
Though reckless and feckless.

The lark has a flair
For lilting on air.

The blackbird's absurd
He's both flutey and fruity.

The eagle is regal
Flying high in the sky.

But the owl is a howl
And a wise auld fowl.

Becalmed

The ocean lies like a great mirror
Flat, dead, calm.
Is Nature asleep?

One longs for movement
To ripple and fill the sails
And break the stillness of the sea-washed air.

Broad beams of light strike deep
Converging into narrow lines
Far below the surface of the sea.

Far far away a fret of waves
Sunbeams skittering like butterflies
Dancing and dazzling in the distance.

During such weather and on such a day
The voracious shark circles
Searching the quiet waters for its prey.

Exquisite mover. Expressionless eyes.
Streamlined, relentless
Dependent on the element of surprise.

Frenzied activity! Turmoil! Splash!
Filed fangs exposed in momentary flash.
The water levels. Composure regained.

And the ocean lies like a great mirror.
Flat, dead, calm.
Is Nature asleep?

Shirley Ohlmeyer
Inishfree Writers

Comparisons

For Christine

Hedge-height
A line of leafless trees
Stand stark
Against a stagnant sky
Dark and thinned
By winter and farmer

Sun breaks through
Piercing yellow rays shoot
From a fresh expense
Of purest blue

I have crossed the sea
Now I am on a bus
Making my way to you

Wisps of cloud like kisses hang

Brittle-fingered branches
Black as pitch
Thick as thieves
Shred waves of brightness
Into staccato beams
That blast the clipped
Crisp field

From its burrow
Brown rabbit bolts
Making for the sunbed
Making a break for it

Wisps of cloud like kisses hang
I am on a bus
Making my way to you

131

Haiku I

My wife
In bed sleeping
Troubles me still

Haiku II

Lager. Even the urine
Of the Gods
Is no small gift

Haiku III

Suddenly, blue tits
Flitting in winter branches
Chasing spring

Haiku IV

To glimpse again
The most revealing light
He enters the dark forest.

Royce Harper
Newtownabbey Writers' Group

Ruairi the Cat Thief

*R*uairi our beautiful Havana cat is a member of the Siamese cat family. We had previously been owned by a Siamese cat called Mistu Issac Edward, affectionately known as Teddy. Teddy suffered a stroke a few months short of his sixteenth birthday. We were devastated and swore that there would never be another cat in our lives. Needless to say that as cat lovers the time came when we realised that we really missed a feline presence in our lives. After much deliberation we decided not to go for a Siamese again because there was no way we could replace Teddy. We wanted a cat with character and also one who would be willing to travel in our camper van.

After a lot of thought and research we settled on a Havana. Ruairi came into our lives when he was twelve weeks old, not only did he have character, he also had an attitude problem. The only word I can use to describe him is wilful, with a capital W. Six foot fences had almost always ensured that Teddy stayed in our large back garden. Not so with Ruairi! It was really quite funny to see this tiny green eyed, brown kitten running up the fence and on to the garage belonging to Janet and Doug, our next door neighbours. He would arrogantly march down their path and enter their conservatory through the cat flap. He was now on territory belonging to Sammy, a beautiful blue eyed, fluffy white kitten who was two weeks Ruairi's senior. Ruairi and Sammy became the best of friends and roamed the neighbourhood. They were always together, playing or fighting, teasing the local dogs or just sleeping in the sunshine. After a while Ruairi started to develop his hunting instinct. Unfortunately for him wild life was thin on the ground in the built up area we lived in, so 'presents' were few and far between. However, Ruairi was not to be beaten. He started to bring home Sammy's toys, no problem we just threw them back over the fence. Then soft toys started to appear. We asked Janet if they were hers, no! We checked with various neighbours to see if perhaps they belonged to their grandchildren, no! The collection was growing, so we asked the local priest if they could have come from the parochial hall, perhaps collected for a garden fete or something, no!

One day he brought home a fluffy hedgehog, it was enormous, at least twelve inches by eight inches. Goodness knows how he got it over the six foot fence, and then carried it through our bungalow to the bedroom as an early morning gift.

About a week later there was a knock on the front door. It was Doug to ask if we had a hedgehog. Janet had bought it as a present for a friend's toddler. She had put it on a high shelf to stop Sammy and Ruairi from taking it to play with. When she went to retrieve it, there it was gone. It didn't take much thought to deduce who the culprit was. How on earth he got it through the cat-flap in their kitchen door and then through the one in their conservatory door defies imagination. The best though was the saga of the slipper. One morning (Ruairi always was an early morning thief) he brought us a brand new turquoise sheepskin moccasin. I assumed that it was Janet's and threw it over the fence. Next day Ruairi brought it back again. This time I put it through Janet's letterbox so that she would see it on her way out of the house to go to work. The next day Ruairi brought it back yet again.

That evening as soon as I heard Janet in her garden I hopped on to a garden bench and called over to her. She was laughing and said I knew that slipper must be to do with Ruairi. I said I've only just noticed that the size on the bottom is 8, and I'll bet you only take a 4. Needless to say we ended up crying with laughter. The slipper hung around in our conservatory, and one day when Ruairi was being a pain I said why don't you go and get the other slipper then I will have a pair. I actually take a size 8. Well believe it, or believe it not the very next morning Ruairi brought me the other slipper.

When we were packing up our home to move to Ireland I decided that there was no way that Ruairi was bringing all his loot with him, he has plenty of his own soft toys. We let him keep the pink panther, and a white cat. The ones he had damaged whilst trying to 'kill' them we binned, and the rest we gave to a cat rescue to sell at their open day. We are now settled in rural Ireland and so far all the presents Ruairi brings are live. I don't know which is worst, but at least I no longer live in fear of getting my collar felt.

Did I hear you say what happened to the slippers? We still have them!

Stephanie Handley
Inishfree Writers

134

The Black Arch

Travelling
Antrim's coast road,
I pass through
that dark arch way,
and out again,
a gateway,
where sea meets rocky cliffs
and white seabirds cry.
Again towards the glens I journey
how many times
I'll never know.
This time it is the autumn of my life
and beneath an autumn sky.

Billy Stewart
Newtownabbey Writers' Group

Brock the Badger

I'm fat and I grunt.
I'm often the brunt
Of division and spite.
Goaded to fight
Throughout the years
I've lived with my fears.
Hunted and baited
Cruelly-fated.

My coat's like a mat
On a body that's fat.
My legs are too short,
Sometimes I shout
As I waddle about
With my black and white snout
That's lethal and long
And incredibly strong.

I'm white and I'm grey
I sleep mostly by day
Nocturnal and shy
I don't really know why.
I'm sort of pathetic
Sad. Macabre. Genetic.
Throwback. Unreal.
So strong — yet so frail.

Crazy Cruit Cows

*O*nce upon a time two cows lived in a field on Cruit Island. Nowadays cows are rare on Cruit and these two took on a sort of a novelty value, to the extent that they were individually named Clarabel and Crantzen. Clarabel and Crantzen led charmed lives.

They had plenty of pasture and a network of small stone-fenced fields in which to browse.

People showed interest in them and they were regarded with some affection.

Sadly, like many overindulged beings they were not happy. They looked at the fields far away in the distance and wished that they could be there.

The two animals were good friends. They stood together, sometimes shoulder to shoulder and gazed into the great beyond. Clarabel was skittish and good-natured, but Crantzen, who was the dominant partner in the relationship, was seriously mean.

She had a huge head like a buffalo's and a Neanderthal brow fringed with tight brown curls. At the sides of her face were two mean eyes, impassive as dead jellyfish. She gave and she asked no quarter.

The Gomer family were their neighbours. Quiet and inoffensive people they were — strangers from across who moved around like shadows and made little impression except for the passion with which they worked their garden, turning it into a work of art. Gentle and unassuming, the Gomers really loved nature and often observed Clarabel and Crantzen across the stone wall.

Imagine their consternation when, one day they looked out to see the two cows wandering over their garden, trampling everything in their path. Mrs Gomer rushed for the broom and charged outside to confront the interlopers. Clarabel and Crantzen regarded her transfixed — this crazed creature in a frenzy of hostility. A bemused look came over Crantzen's face. She lowered her head, rolled her eyes, snorted and ... Mrs Gomer moved fast — back into the house whence she had come. Clarabel and Crantzen followed her to the house, left their cards and jumped back into their field.

That evening they watched the Gomers as they replaced stones on the wall and fussed about in their garden.

Now they had got a taste for the good life and the next day, Clarabel and Crantzen jumped the stone wall again. The Gomers had gone out for the day and nobody tried to stop them. What a jolly time they had! They devastated the plants, demolished the flowers, knocked down the clothes line, trampled the lobster pots and tossed the turf stack. They even ate the letters out of the letter box. Evidence of where the miscreants had been was everywhere. If ever cows deserved to die, they did.

But the Gomers were kind-hearted and long-suffering people and asked for clemency for the offenders when their owners offered to get rid of them. More fencing was done and an uneasy peace ensued.

Clarabel and Crantzen often eyed the garden where they had been so happy and longed to return there. Now that there was a ferocious interest in them, they felt really restricted. At last they could bear it no longer. Under cover of darkness, they decided to make their move. They headed for Gomers', intent on investigating every inch of the property right up to the front door, into the shed, over the paths, down the steps — everywhere — leaving a wake of destruction behind them.

It never even entered their heads that the Gomers might be frightened out of their wits as they lay in their beds, by all the snuffling, scraping, fumbling and heavy breathing going on outside in the dark. They thought their hour had come.

The morning dawned fine and clear, but a storm was brewing. There was an uncanny stillness in the charged atmosphere. For the first time ever, Clarabel and Crantzen had second thoughts about what they had done and were beset by terrible feelings of remorse and uneasiness.

It was with a desperate sense of foreboding that they watched the big transporter lorry slowly snake along the winding roads of Cruit towards where they stood …

Shirley Ohlmeyer
Inishfree Writers

138

Stella

An excerpt from **Spricks**

Skid would rise at seven o'clock in the morning, leave home at a quarter past and hope to be at the monastery in time for the eight o'clock mass. His journey would take him through the very centre of Belfast which was thronged with working men. There seemed to be countless thousands of them in their dark working clothes and flat caps and a cigarette dangling from their mouths. The trams would be filled to overflowing with workers hanging on to every piece of protruding metal or wood. There must have been more people standing in the aisles, on the stairs and landing platform than were actually sitting down. Some would even stand on the back bumper outside the tram and the conductor would have to reach out the window to collect their fares. As the overloaded trams clanked noisily away towards Queen's Bridge Skid would slip into Castle Street to board a trolley bus. The trolley buses were beautiful, they were warm, quiet, clean and quick and there was always two or three of them waiting to glide up the Falls Road. They would be virtually empty on the outward journey so he could take his favourite seat, which was on the upper deck at the top of the stairs; this enabled him to monitor the movements in the mirror of the conductor and everyone who boarded or left the bus and allowed him to have a peaceful smoke without some oul doll telling him it would stunt his growth. His own family seemed to be the only people who didn't smoke. Although cigarettes were called cancer sticks or coffin nails and just about every adult used tobacco it was a serious business for an underage smoker to be caught in the act.

Skid had a special dispensation to leave his altar boy clothes in the sacristy so he didn't have to lug his small case around with him. He just had a small thin canvas school bag suspended from his shoulder by a long thin strap. He hated it and envied other boys who had real leather or even sturdy ex-army knapsack type school bags that stayed on your back out of the way. But there was really no need for a school bag, all the text books were kept in school. The contents of his bag were an Irish language book of very poor quality, his homework jotter and a couple of rounds of soggy jam sandwiches. The bus would slow down at the top of Lower Clonard Street, Skid would hop off, check the time on the clock of Farry's Pub, and head up Clonard Street.

Skid bounded up the stairs of the trolley bus hoping to dive into his favourite seat just to the left of the top of the curving staircase. He was already reaching into his pocket for his five Woodbine and matches. He almost sat on top of a dark lady who was already there. Discountenanced he took a seat two rows up across the aisle. The stranger posed a problem. Should he light a cigarette in the presence of an adult? He would hardly see this stranger again. She was unlikely to tout to any of the authority figures — she wouldn't know any of them. He decided to take the chance. He lit up. His cigarette was in his mouth and he was using the sandpapered edge of the match box to file the nicotine stains off his fingers. This filing process hurt but it was the only way to avoid detection. He thought of the advantages. If he ever committed a crime the police could never trace him because his fingerprints were virtually rubbed away. Then he thought of the oul doll behind him who had pinched his seat. This definitely was a disadvantage of living in Belfast. "So cosmopolitan," his sister Petronilla liked to say, "why you even get people from as far away as Ballymena and Bangor."

"Hey, kid."

Skid froze. Was she talking to him? She, as an adult, had no right to use such a slang term that only kids and Americans used. Did she thing his ma was a goat? More importantly was she going to tell him off? Skid turned slowly and apprehensively.

His downcast eyes lighted on her high heeled shoes. There was a thin gold chain on her left ankle. His eyes travelled up her suntanned legs and stopped at her knees. Her legs were crossed. Ladies didn't cross their legs. Rosie was forever telling his sisters that it was unladylike and immodest.

"Me?" he asked.

"Yes, you, there's nobody else here, is there?"

"What do you want?" he sullenly inquired.

"A light please?" she airily asked.

Skid was puzzled. She didn't fit into any of the two categories of Belfast females — wee dames who were forever touting on him, or oul dolls who were always telling him off. She seemed to be in a category all of her own. She wasn't as old as his ma nor as young as his sisters. Skid rose and approached warily. She had green eyes with what looked like little flames in their depths. Her heart shaped face was framed with lustrous hair that caught the morning sunlight streaming through the window of the bus and seemed to surround her head with a glow more radiant than the soup-plate halos of the saints on the monastery walls.

She was smiling warmly at him and laughed as she said, "You're certainly not one of the Ovalteenys, more of a nicoteeny."

Skid blushed deeply. She uncrossed her legs as he approached. He was standing between her golden knees as he proffered the lighted match. The inside of her knees touched the outside of his bare legs as he leant forward and he felt himself tremble and blush even more deeply. He looked into her eyes. The little flames were flecks of gold that seemed to dance.

She looked into his eyes steadily while inhaling her cigarette. "Am I on the right bus for the Royal Victoria Hospital?"

"Yes," blurted Skid, "it's the stop after mine."

"Sit down beside me," she said invitingly, "I don't know my way round Belfast. My father is in the hospital and I'm staying with my aunt near the university. I live in Derry."

Skid's mind and his emotions raced. He felt uncomfortable yet strangely happy and definitely tongue tied.

"What's your name?" she asked.

"Willie... Willie John." He was suddenly aware of what a grubby, ordinary back street kid he was. He thought she would be called Esmeralda like Quasimodo's girlfriend and he was beginning to feel more like Quasimodo.

"I'm Stella," she said.

"I knew it," he thought. *Stella* meaning *star*, as in *Stella Maris*, except that she should be *Star of the mountains, the skies and the sea*.

"Stella Shields," she continued.

"Thank God for that," he thought. "Didn't he know an oul doll called Shields, and wasn't there a Shield's Street up the road?" At least part of her belonged to the world he knew. He looked out the window and saw the bus was at Alma Street. Two more stops and he would have to alight and this apparition would be lost forever. In desperation he said, "Will you wait for me?"

"What do you mean?"

"I mean wait for me until I grow up and marry you."

"Sure," she laughed.

Skid felt like an idiot. What had made him say that? Did it hark back to the time when the lovely Oonah, who worked in Trainor's dress

141

shop, had asked him would he marry her when he grew up and he had said yes? Or again when the big millie had grabbed him outside McCaun's butchers shop, held him aloft in triumph to her work mates, then clutched him to her greasy bosom and asked, "Will you marry me when you grow up?" "I will, I will," he had readily agreed.

Now here he was doing the same stupid thing.

Overcome by his own feelings of inadequacy he stood up and sheepishly said, "It's my stop. I'm away," and bolted down the stairs imagining he heard her silvery laugh tinkle down after him. As usual he jumped off the trolley bus as it slowed down, and collided with a pole which he usually didn't. The bus drove on.

Skid didn't do a button of good that day whether it was the Stella effect or the bang on his head.

Bill Hatton
Newtownabbey Writers' Group

Jimmy

*I*t was the rambling rose that clinched it.

Jimmy was eighty-five, the same age as the century, and he lived on his own. He had tried sharing each of his married children's homes in turn after his wife's death three years earlier, but felt an intruder in the lives of the sons and daughters he had guided through childhood. He wanted independence. He had always had a fierce pride in self-reliance, that had never left him since his early days of a hard-fought existence in West Belfast. A home help twice a week was all he needed — until his eyesight faded and he could see little more than shadows.

As a result of his deteriorating vision his eldest daughter encouraged, cajoled and pleaded with him to take up residence in Avon House a council-run home for senior citizens, where she could keep an eye on him, living as she did only five minutes away. His rebellious nature fought against it. He had a quirky sense of humour, could be belligerent, argumentative and generously loyal in turn. The most he could concede was one day a week at Avon House for lunch, an afternoon's bingo, and a check on his health. 'You won't catch me living with a load of old people waiting for the grave' he declared in uncompromising mood, and an unmistakable Belfast accent, to the sons and daughters he still refused to live with.

But that was before the rambling rose.

Avon House had its share of eccentric characters even before Jimmy's once a week visits. Harriet was a lady in her seventies, always on the move. She walked slowly with determined strides around the main lounge and corridors of the building. Visitors would often find the entrance to Avon House locked when they came to visit their relatives. On ringing the bell Harriet would open the door and insist that she did not allow strangers into 'her house'. She once proposed to Jimmy, and after his refusal of marriage never spoke to him again.

Hans was a German resident. Tall, thin, unsmiling, with military bearing, the rimless spectacles reminiscent of World War Two prisoner of war camp commandants. A fresh air fanatic, he was observed by

Jimmy to follow in Harriet's relentless footsteps, opening every window in all weathers as he went.

Jimmy had for many years been an enthusiastic, compulsive, gardener. It was this fact that eventually persuaded him that two days rather than one would be better for him to join the 'ancients', as he called them, of Avon House. The gardens were tended by professional, but less than dedicated, council gardeners, and even with his limited vision Jimmy knew that the rambling rose was in a worse state of health than any of the human residents. He let the staff know that *he* understood the science of soil composition, the correct way to prune, and which fertilisers to use. The staff smiled as Jimmy came twice a week to attend to the horticultural needs of 'his' rose.

Julie, the warden of Avon House, was an efficient woman in her late thirties, with a sympathetic understanding of her elderly charges. She had taken a distinct liking to Jimmy, her 'weekly octogenarian', his refusal to accept the difficulties of age reminding her of the Welsh poet Dylan Thomas's lines about his father's age — 'Fight, fight, against the dying of the light'. She gently hinted that the yellow rambler had improved so much under Jimmy's ministrations that perhaps two days a week were not enough to ensure its fully perfumed summer glory.

That is how Jimmy became a leading light amongst the characters of Avon House. Julie in her official capacity kept a fondly amused, benign watch on him, as on all her 'family'. She smiled in the early evenings as she watched Harriet on her slow-paced travels, followed by Hans breathing deeply as he opened all the windows in turn. And Jimmy a few steps behind — closing them.

Jimmy quickly settled down to life in Avon House. Its routine he blatantly ignored. His philosophy of a happy life was to avoid order and regimentation of any kind. 'Institutionalised' was a condition and a word that would never apply to him. His confident air, which became stronger the more he felt unsure of himself, gave him a place unique in the annals of the retirement home; regarded by the staff almost as a colleague and by the residents as a person apart.

Many of the ladies who looked after the 50 elderly citizens confided in him their family troubles, their hopes and their fears. Unhappy marriages, unruly teenagers, financial worries; his humour, perception and advice was equal to all problems.

Jimmy revelled in his role as father confessor. And in truth if you looked into his clear, penetratingly blue eyes, you would not have thought that the penetration was more an understanding of the human

144

condition than of physical sight. He could see very little, and was often sad in his quiet moments, missing the remembered pleasures of reading, and the faces of his wife and family as they enjoyed life together in past years.

When Harriet tired of her separate patrolling of the rooms and passages, one day marching out of Avon House altogether into the streets on a fine summer afternoon. She was missing for two hours before her absence was noticed. Then alarm was in the air. Jimmy, with supreme control in the emergency, calmly offered to go in search of her. Julie, the warden, almost let him go on the mission before remembering with her usual smile that this ebullient old man with his self-assured personality could hardly see a foot in front of him, never mind seeking the wandering Harriet. At this moment Harriet strode in, completely oblivious of the administrative panic she had caused.

Jimmy continued to tend his rose. He also assumed responsibility for a tomato plant that was in a terminal state in the conservatory leading to the rear garden. He knew all about tomatoes and their needs. He seemed to know just about everything on every subject that could be acquired during the lifetime of an enquiring mind. Avon House was not used to this type of guest. The elderly and infirm came her to spend their last days being cared for in quiet stillness and peace. Jimmy had other ideas.

He explored and became familiar with this surroundings. Avon House could be likened to a planet with five satellites, the planet being the main central lounge which could hold a large crowd at the Christmas Party or Hallowe'en Night celebrations. From this hub five corridors led to five smaller lounges each giving ten people the illusion of a private family home. These rooms each had a dining table, television and armchairs. They were bright with flowers and pictures; from there a passage led to private rooms with bed, wash basin, personal ornaments and photographs. Together with a large kitchen and administrative office at the main entrance this was Jimmy's new home.

He handed in his pension book and received in return a few pounds' pocket money every Thursday, his pay day.

A dark-haired petite woman who seemed to bustle around in a disorganised fashion, but was anything but disorganised, was in charge of coach excursions, summer outings and the social events for both occupants of Avon House and their visitors. She was certainly efficient at collecting the 50 pence contribution every Thursday. Jimmy flatly refused to contribute. 'I'm not gallivanting around the countryside with oul' ones too far gone to hold a decent conversation' was his final comment on the subject. However, he changed his mind when he heard that a day at Ascot races was planned.

Yes, he still had his camel hair coat, his dark glasses, his trilby hat — *and* his binoculars. They would not be of any practical use with the state of his eyes, but he would cut a dashing figure amongst the racing fraternity. His excited anticipation was boundless. In his imagination he could hear the cheering crowds, the pounding crescendo of hooves. Great heavens! He could almost see the jockey's brilliantly coloured silks. He sighed contentedly. Between his thriving rose, the recovering tomato plant, his social status amongst carers and cared for, he began to believe that life in Avon House had its compensations.

During the week prior to the great race day he listened avidly as his son Brian, on his regular Wednesday evening visit, read the lists of runners and riders, their weights and form, from the columns of the *Sporting Life.* Brian was as enthusiastic as his father. He was delighted at the old man's renewed interest in life and proud too that so many people thought highly of the man he had respected and loved all his life.

The day of the Ascot outing dawned. Jimmy, looking like a television sports racing commentator, was rejuvenated, resplendent as he joined the waiting coach.

How are the mighty fallen.

Jimmy had misunderstood Margaret's announcement of the Ascot trip. The coach had been hired to take the residents on a thrilling visit to the newly-built giant Asda hypermarket five miles away. The only racing Jimmy could envisage was dashing with a shopping trolley between stacked rows of washing powder, tinned peas and pet food.

Jimmy did not go.

Instead he dwelt upon the vagaries and disappointments of life as he sprayed his rambling rose with insecticide. Venting his frustrations on greenfly and promising himself that this evening he would shut the windows with an extra vigour — ten seconds after Hans had opened them.

Avon House was situated in a wide avenue with open green lawns along its length, regularly and neatly moved by the city council parks department. The entire avenue was the latest thing in town planning. It had an air of spaciousness. It was the perfection of contemporary housing estates. Indeed one would hardly be aware that it *was* part of a housing estate with semi-detached individually designed and discreetly placed to the eastern side of the avenue. It was quiet, even on weekdays a Sunday peacefulness could be felt. There was little traffic, so that Jimmy with his limited visitor was quite safe strolling from the safety of the retirement home to either end of the road.

This was fortunate for both ends held their individual attractions for him. If he turned right on leaving Avon House he could make his way to *The Raven*, an ancient hostelry with a relaxed atmosphere where he was regarded by the local patrons with affection. He was as much a character in *The Raven* as in Avon House itself. This was his escape from institutional life, he declared. It provided his regular few hours of normality away from the foibles of the aged. He could never class himself with them despite his 85 years. *The Raven* was roomy, comfortable old-fashioned with a long bar of mellow oak. There would be no plastic-tabled invasion of this venerable inn.

The other end of the avenue was Jimmy's alternative evening rendezvous. The *Tiger Moth* was a modern state of the art brewery owned premises. If one was confused by its name in lights on the outside a visit to its interior would only increase the confusion. In the lounge bar the walls were adorned with coloured photographs of the *Tiger Moth* twin-engined aeroplanes of an earlier generation, some in action with mounted machine guns, others in glorious free flight above dazzling sun-touched clouds. These flying machines looked down upon luxurious thick pile carpets, plastic tables and sophisticated red dralon seating. Musak and the hum of conversation mingled with the gentle exchanges of courting couples. The *Tiger Moth* bar room also had its touch of luxury. It was distinguished from the lounge by its pool table and television. And the pictures. They were Tiger Moths, but they were butterflies. The drinker with an interest in nature study could have his fill of their coloured glory gazing from the walls in motionless flight.

The Raven and *Tiger Moth* with their differing clientele gave a balance to Jimmy's life, together with his rambling rose and philosophic observations of ageing humanity in Avon House. He viewed Harriet's incessant parade and Hans' fresh air fanaticism with wry amusement; but by far his favourite performance was enacted each evening by a lady rarely seen at any other time. She was extremely large and everyone was immediately aware of her presence as she instinctively made a dramatic entrance. Even before her appearance she could be heard, in the wings as it were, seemingly in the agonised throes of a long-forgotten tragedy. In a voluminous floral tent of a dress which emphasised rather than concealed a vast amount of quivering flesh she had all the qualities of a Greek ampitheatre goddess. In the depths of her wailing she was supported by a chorus of three acolytes; thin wails of women who together would not equal the weight of the tragedian. They moaned a low point of sympathetic harmony to the grief of a past shrouded in mystery.

Jimmy, who had been a keen reader of Charles Dickens, named this vision Miss Havisham. She evoked in his imagination scenes of a deserted wedding feast, vanished bridegroom, crumbling multi-tiered wedding cake and a bride in abandoned distraction.

Miss Havisham of Avon House revelled in the passion of some dimly-distant betrayal. Describing the performance to his two sons he would revert to the vernacular of his West Belfast youth. 'Them four oul' dolls,' he would say, 'relics of oul' dacency.'

Having taken keen interest in the evening performance of Miss Havisham and company, Jimmy would shake his head at the infinite variety of human behaviour. Horticulture was much more reliably predictable. He would then retire to the privacy of his room, wash, put on his camel hair overcoat, adjust his hat to a slightly rakish angle on the Kildare side, and saunter forth to either *The Raven* or *Tiger Moth*.

A Donegal Ghost Story

The commercial rush of pre-Christmas shopping was too much for me. The panic-buying last minute multitudes made the crowded stores claustrophobic. My antidote to the mass hysteria of present-searching humanity was to get in the car and head for an area of Donegal guaranteed to calm shattered nerves with its quiet rural peace and the even tenor of life which seemed to mock the frantic festivities of 1998 and the looming approach of a new millennium.

I drove through the bargain-hunting traffic jams of Letterkenny, and avoiding the even worse grid-locked vehicles of Derry city, took the turn from Burnfoot into the remote hush that is the peninsula of Inishowen. It was a crisply cold day with a watery December sun. As I passed through quiet villages, past the turn to Inch Island, I felt childhood memories rekindled by sight of Christmas trees brightly lit in the windows of warmly-inviting cottages and houses. Taverns were advertising 'turkey and ham dinners by candlelight' and, just as in my native Rosses, every passer-by would wave an innocent smile of friendship for the stranger. The warm glow of remembered Christmases, poorer financially than the money-seeking and spendthrift Nineties, but much richer in the simple pleasures of the holy season, brought recollections of friends and relations long-departed.

This feeling of wellbeing as I drove along the quiet roads of Inishowen was a *prelude to an experience that I can only describe as supernatural.*

You must understand that I did not believe in ghosts, poltergeists or the death-heralding of the banshee; tales of which sent us from fireside terror to pull bedclothes over our heads in the days of Tir na Nog. No! This was the close of the 20th Century. The fears engendered by shadows of candle and gas lamp had disappeared with electric light. In spite of this reasoning my Inishowen visit brought me to a realisation that there are indeed more things in heaven and earth than my limited philosophy encompassed.

I stopped for lunch at Moran's Hotel in Carndonough, a typical small Donegal town which a flurry of snow had turned into a Dickensian Christmas card. After an enjoyable meal in the old-fashioned dining room (I had sole beautifully cooked and served with the courtesy of bygone days, deliberately avoiding the turkey and plum pudding until the day itself). I paid my bill at the hotel's reception area. There I noticed an advertisement for the local bookshop. 'The largest stock of antiquarian, secondhand and new books in the North West' it proclaimed. And they were having a pre-Christmas sale. I was hooked. Books have long been my passion; bookshops places where hours passed by unnoticed. This was a day to escape from glittering Christmas gift malls into the intensely quiet pleasure of literary delights.

The bookshop passed all my expectations. A warren of rooms with bookshelves floor to ceiling; stepladders to reach otherwise inaccessible volumes. The warmth of the book-lined rooms was equalled by the enthusiasm and knowledge of the owner. He claimed to have an unrivalled 'rare and antiquarian' collection, but in truth there was everything from bundles of 1920s *Tatler* and *Ireland's Own* magazines to first editions of William Allingham's poetry; from paperback early orange Penguins to leather-bound volumes of *Punch*. I had discovered a secondhand heaven and I doubted whether a single afternoon would be enough to explore its treasures.

Nevertheless I came away as the bookseller was closing for the night, with but one volume, and later wished that I had never visited Carndonough. *I never will again.*

My solitary purchase was one of the volumes which appeared to be new. It WAS new, its pages unturned. The cover illustration had fired my imagination, had made my choice inevitable, ominously so as it turned out. A graveyard scene in moonlight which reminded me of the Bronte burial place at Howarth on the bleak Yorkshire Moors. It showed evocative ivy-covered gravestones, eerily suggestive, with lichen-obscured inscriptions. The artist had highlighted one grave with a mysteriously illegible epitaph. The book's title was *Tomorrow and Tomorrow and Tomorrow*. I recognised Shakespeare's words from *Macbeth* having been a devoted reader of the Bard for many years.

The author, Alan J P Mayne was a writer new to me. I looked forward to getting home to the Rosses and immersing myself over Christmas with the latest addition to my library.

Reading in bed is one of life's greatest pleasures, and this book gripped my interest into the small hours. The opening chapter told the early schoolday adventures of the hero; of his first days during which the teacher gave her young pupils four simple additions. Those with four correct answers to be rewarded with a sweet. The boy who featured throughout the novel not only had his four correct answers, he amazed the teacher by handing in five. How could a six-year-old invent an extra problem? This episode amazed and delighted me.

It was an exact replica of my own earliest school memory. I had often wondered about it as I grew into adulthood. This writer had experienced the same phenomenon.

As I read further an uneasiness stirred within me. The boy, now in his late teens, and secretly infatuated with a serene and seemingly unapproachable girl of great beauty, dreams of his love and wakes shouting her name. His parents, brothers and sisters rush to his room. As he comes out of his dream he hears his father's voice. 'You must have had a nightmare, you woke us all up calling your sister's name.' His sister had the same name as the girl in his dream. He said nothing, relieved that his longing for his secret love was still his secret.

I could not believe what I was reading. This had been my secret too. Yet here it was in another man's fiction. The author again quoted Shakespeare: 'She never told her love, but let concealment, like a worm i'the bud, feed on her damask cheeks.'

My unease turned to foreboding. Here was a mirror of my own life, an account written by ... I turned to the cover again. Alan J P Mayne. AJPM. *My own initials.* I looked at the graveyard scene once more. The engraved lettering on the tombstone was clearly legible and clear of lichen. *Requiescant in Pace. AJPM.* I must not have looked carefully enough before. As I held the book in bed dread turned to panic. I flung the book into the shadows at the far corner of the room. Was this another nightmare? Was I really awake?

Morning dawned and with it sanity returned. Coincidence I told myself. A book of my life written by a stranger. Ridiculous! In the clear light of day with the sun shining coldly on a bright covering of powdery snow, birds singing as they searched for crumbs and berries, the terrors of the night evaporated. I took the book from the corner where it lay and replaced it on my bedside shelf.

The following two nights I read, and what I read was an account of all my years. Thoughts, plans and desires that had passed through my mind, but secretly, disclosed to no living soul, were here recorded. It was unreal — yet too real. My mind whirled with the impossibility of the atmosphere created by this book. My stomach felt queasy, yet hollow. The words of the ghost of Hamlet's father came into my mind...

'I could a tale unfold whose lightest word would harrow up thy

151

soul.' I lay in bed transfixed, unable to stop reading until I reached the last word of the last paragraph. I felt an air of evil permeating the night around me. Nightmare or madness? Logic failed me as I tried desperately to hold onto reality. There had to be an explanation. Turning to the title pages I saw that it was a first novel, typeset in 10 on 11 point Baskerville type. First published December 1998.

December 1998!

It must be a printing error. Looking again at the graveyard depicted on the cover I could see that the marble stone had no longer a covering of ivy. The epitaph was deeply etched and could be clearly read in its entirety:

I HAD SIX MONTHS TO LIVE!

Arthur McCaffrey
Inishfree Writers

Teenagers

A Monologue

Scene: A man sits in his home, upstairs in his study
Time: The present

*T*his is my birthday. I'm 50 today.

Gawd! it's downhill all the way now. But does anyone care? No. Not even a card from either of them this morning. Just a quick 'Half a century today, Dad' as the front door slammed. Very funny, ha, bloody ha!

They probably only realised it was my birthday when they saw the card from their mother sitting on the breakfast table. Not that they sit down for breakfast, anyway. Apparently it's the in thing to wolf down food while you're standing. You make a quicker exit that way.

The teenagers of today are an ungrateful lot. They don't appreciate the sacrifices you make for them. It's not like it was in my youth. We had respect for our parents, and respect for the home, too. It wasn't treated like some bloody hotel.

It's like bedlam here in the mornings.

Hours spent in the bathroom, gallons of unused hot water going down the drain, with shouts of *Where's my...? Who's moved my...?* and all the while the turmoil is spreading from upstairs to downstairs.

When the bathroom is finally free, you find towels left hanging on the floor. Dirty linen lying *beside* the laundry basket. Toothpaste tubes, squeezed in the middle, left capless. I've never seen such a conglomeration of hair products in my life. In my day a Brylcreem wave was enough. As for sweet wrappers. Who the hell eats sweets in the bathroom, I ask you?

Then there's the food. You'd need an E.C. subsidy for that!

Just look at the size of that bloody bill! Friday is shopping day, by Monday the fridge is empty. How can they get through all that food and still look like stick insects? And the takeaways! Chinese, Italian,

European, you name it, they'll eat it. The whole house reeks of the stuff. Complaints of stomach ache the next day. They had it coming, that's what I say.

The kids of today never take advice from anybody, well certainly not from me anyway. I've been told 'You make *your own* decisions, dad.' Who me? I'm a married man with two teenage sons!

How the hell did they pass their English exams?

They sound illiterate. Can't hold a decent conversation. They mutter at you, sentences are limited to *Yeah, yeah, Nice one, Cool, man, That's where I'm at*, or, *Get a life!*

Try watching a decent programme on television.

The remote control comes into action and you're now stuck with *Top of the Pops* or the *Pepsi Charts*. When you make a remark, just the kind of remark anyone would make about a song that doesn't have a tune or sensible lyrics, the response is to adapt a sullen pose, or stamp off with mutters of *Get with it* or *Nobody understands me*.

I bought a computer to get away from it all.

I had the Internet installed, too. Never made a worse buy in my life! Now they're Internetting all over the place. You should see my bloody phone bill. That thing is being disconnected for sure. There's going to be changes in this house!

As for their friends. Gawd!

There's that gormless looking creature who moves at action replay speed. He wears a baseball cap and apparently doesn't know where the front of his head is.

You take my John; he knocks about with a right touchy prat, who took umbrage because I made a perfectly innocent remark about the ring in his nose. It's time John got himself a girlfriend, anyway. I hope he's not abnormal or something.

And look at that tart Michael brought home.

Skirt up to her backside and a hairstyle that defied gravity. Cinderella's slipper wouldn't fit on that one, that's for sure. But you daren't say anything or you'll hear *Nobody else's dad gets on like you* and mutterings about somebody called *Victor Meldrew*.

You take this house late at night.

That's when you suffer the torture of sleep deprivation. You've just settled into sleep when there's BANG, SLAM, THUMP, and kitchen

154

noises.

They've just been out for a meal for Gawd's sake!

Then *clump, clump* on the stairs.

'Do something,' my wife says.

'Do WHAT?'

'Something,' she says succinctly.

Still, that's not as bad as when the phone rings at 1 a.m. It's always bad news, too.

They need a lift home.

There's sure to be a 100 mph gale and a warning of poor visibility and black ice. Do I get any thanks? No.

There's usually a remark. 'I'm freezing. What kept you?'

What is that flaming racket going on outside? I'll have to take a look.

There's quite a number of cars in the avenue. Would you just look at those handsome well-dressed lads. Why can't mine dress like that? But, no, they'd rather be in leather, slung about with chains and metal zips. Where have I gone wrong?

There's a guy getting out of one of the cars who reminds me of Ron Turner. Haven't seen Ron in years. He was a great friend. That's what family responsibility does. It breaks up friendships. Well, I'm just going to ring Ron tomorrow. Look after my own interests for a change.

Hey, wait a minute! They're all coming up my driveway.

Gawd, I don't believe it!

Those handsome well-dressed lads are mine! What the Hell have they done now? Must rush downstairs and hear the bad news.

What's happening here?

Why... it is Ron... and Tommy... and Brian, and... Can't hear myself think for all this noise.

'Surprise. Surprise!'

'Happy Birthday!'

'Gee, guys, it's great to see you all.' (Dear God, I've got a lump in my throat.)

'No, I didn't know anything about it. The boys know I'm not one for celebrating birthdays.'

'Yes, Ron, I am proud of them. I must say we've been blessed. My two are very thoughtful. They've never given us a moment's worry. They're at University now, you know. — But what about your own lads? Bet they've grown into great teenagers as well...'

Sarah Barrett

Newtownabbey Writers' Group

155

Liebe

Nicht ahnte ich diese Kraft
diese unsagbare Macht.
nicht wußte ich von
   Verzweiflung
nicht von dieser Tiefe
als ich sie spürte:
die Liebe!
die Iangsam
ins dunkle Erdenreich der
   Sinne
Sich tief verwurzelt
Doch fühle ich Welten in mir
Sonnenlicht durchflutet,
ich fühle mich so Ieicnt,
als hätte Gott micn berührt,
als ich sie empfing:
Die Liebe.

Love

I didn't foresee this energy
This inexpressible power
I didn't know of this
   desperation
Not about this depth
When I felt it:
Love!
Which slowly —
Into the dark domain of the
   senses
Is deeply rooted
But I feel worlds in me,
Sunlight flooded!
I feel so light
As if God had touched me
When I received it:
Love!

Heidi Schulz
Inishfree Writers

On our visit to Donegal, the simplicity and lack of pretension of people impressed me. This was especially true of those who lived on Inishfree. They really seemed to have got their priorities right. This is in direct contrast to the materialism and outward show exhibited by some of us in the North. This story is a tongue-in-cheek look at the latter way of life.

A Dinner of Leftovers

*P*enelope Smythe (with an E), was for a long time my mentor, and who better to advise and instruct than Penelope, of the immaculate home and exquisite taste.

Things ran smoothly in Penny's house. Her children never left a mark on the Laura Ashley wallpaper or the Persian rugs, shoes were regimentally left outside the front door and a beautifully typewritten rota insured that chores were democratically shared. The cats wouldn't have dreamt of peeing indoors, and as for snagging the upholstery, well felines of such rare breeding just didn't.

Jasper, Conrad, Felicity and Hope, the Smythe children, were of course doing splendidly in their Grammar schools, high achievers all of them. Sometimes I'd look at my Billy, my Darren and my Tracey, struggling along, albeit happily at their local secondary shcool and I'd ask myself where did I go wrong?

Well, I knew really, because Penny had put me right.

'They should have gone to Prep school, Sarah, or had extra coaching before the transfer test' she said. That way they would have been assured of a place at a decent school. You know it really is worth it. It will look so much better on a C.V. in years to come.'

To digress, it was Penelope who decided that large families were 'in' in our area, but then again Penny had turned child-bearing into an art form. I wish I'd known about epidurals, water births, plants and soft music when I was panting and screaming my way through my labour intensive lot.

Penny's kids, sorry, children, were born stress-free, in a controlled environment.

157

'A truly uplifting experience' as she often told us girls, in her beautifully modulated voice. And Penelope's babies were all breast-fed of course. She didn't chicken out, as I did, in the face of screeching dissatisfied infants, and reach for the bottle, in more ways than one.

In this, as in many other things, Penny despaired of me; however I used to comfort myself with the fact that the Penelopes of this world needed people like me, as a foil to set them off. It's always good to serve a useful purpose.

About one week after each birth, immaculately dressed, with flaw-less figure, Penelope would sweep into our church, carrying her latest production to be christened. Her husband would bring up the rear with spotless siblings. We female parishioners would look at our spare tires and shapeless outfits and sigh. 'How does she do it?'

But of course we knew. It was a combination of organization, ruthless exercise, and rigid diet, as she often told us. And it goes without saying that no meat, fish, or fowl, ever found its way down Smythe gullets. Penelope's children weren't given sweets, cakes, crisps, or biscuits and the consequences would have been severe had she ever found out that they slipped into our house occasionally to indulge.

Be that as it may, Penelope was quite tolerant of us lesser mortals, who didn't have her will-power. She even brought round a cake, sorry, gateau, when my husband Andrew died suddenly, five years ago, and only sighed heavily when she found out that his insurance would barely cover his funeral expenses let alone keep us in luxury for the rest of our lives.

To give her due, Penelope kept in touch through our lean and hungry years till I muddled my way into a new career, though I always felt that my poverty was a source of great trial to her. I think she felt that I was lowering the tone of the neighbourhood somewhat when I couldn't afford to paint the outside of the house, or keep abreast of the latest fashions and she even suggested on more than one occasion that I should look for something 'a bit more manageable.' It was obvious that she couldn't understand either my incurable optimism that 'some-thing would turn up', or my laid back attitude to money matters.

Concerning financial affairs, Andrew and I had been in agreement.

'Better a dinner of herbs where love is, than a fatted ox and hatred within,' he used to say. He was fond of Biblical quotations was my Andrew, and we brought our children up on liberal dollops of love and laughter, with their baked beans and fish fingers.

Andrew hadn't believed in 'keeping up with the Jones'

'Give people room enough to fit in with you,' he used to say. But honestly, when I used to look at Penelope's beautiful house with its interesting paintings, dust free mahogany and rosewood, sparkling crystal and imaginative flower arrangements, I used to feel the teeniest bit envious.

Penny always had a daily woman and a gardener. She liked to create employment for the less fortunate, she used to tell us, and she offered me a job as well, just after Andrew died. Well, she was a busy woman, what with her golf, her bridge, her committee meetings and her quilting classes.

I didn't mind helping out at Penelope's little soirees and intimate little dinner parties, (though I steadfastly refused her attempts to make me wear a uniform). It was after all a chance for me to try out my Cordon Bleu cooking experience at someone else's expense. And it was to be the start of a whole new career for me, for, though Penelope always refused to let any of her friends poach me, her husband had no such scruples and even ran up some business cards for me, on his computer.

'Sarah,' Penelope would drawl, when I had produced a particularly good Avocado Mousse or Creme Brulee, 'is such a treasure. I'm so lucky to have found her, and no you can't have her phone number I'm keeping her all to myself.' And all the while, Uel would be surreptitiously passing the cards round under the table.

Uel was quite long suffering, I used to think. He was christened Samuel, but quite early on in the marriage Penny decided that 'Uel' had a better ring to it, and that was that. He never seemed to take his wife too seriously, a fact that irritated her considerably. Sometimes, when she was expounding on some particular topic at a dinner party where I was catering, he would catch my eye and wink, or lift his eyes to heaven with that lovely smile hovering about his lips.

Uel was a tower of strength to me in the early days of my business, helping me transport my catering equipment from house to house when I couldn't always afford to run a car. No matter how great the distance or how late I had to work, I only had to phone him on his mobile and he'd be there to help. It was our little secret of course.

I often think back to those days now, when I arrive home from a particularly hectic catering engagement in my own little customised van, and survey the chaos, which is my home nowadays, and sometimes I wonder what became of Penelope. Sadly I'm no longer on her mailing list, though we do hear from time to time of the children, who are making their mark on the world, as are mine, curiously enough.

'I wonder if Penny is still giving those wonderful parties, and keeping such a tidy home and garden these days.' I said to my new husband the other day, as I looked at the newspapers, coffee cups and whiskey glasses that littered our lounge. I had arrived home from work exhausted. He was obviously hoping I had brought something home with me to feed him. 'Penny was always so organized, so much in control, didn't you admire her for that?'

'No, not a bit of it,' said my Sam, easing himself further into the armchair, planting his stockinged feet on the dog, and sinking yet another whiskey. 'This suits me much more. Better a dinner of leftovers in a semi, than a Mercedes in the garage, and hatred within.'

I looked at him in dismay and thought: *Honestly! Penelope's Ex is becoming such a slob these days!*

Margaret Ardill
Newtownabbey Writers' Group

Intervention

Out of the dark,
Back to the dark.
No light between —
Only a few snatched heartbeats.

Now an age of breaking down,
Returning to the matrix.
Muscle and bone to humus,
Molecules to atoms.

We saw the other side of your darkness,
We saw the light you did not see —
It was blood and pain,
Grunting, sweating at the taut lines
Your body the rag tied in the war rope.
Your death the line we fought to
Stamp and go from.

What have you missed?
The sun, the moon, the meadow
And the Knife.

Now you lie in earth's Intervention
Whilst your mother
Harvests another body
From the grass.

Inishfree — the way home

I stumble through mud, the uneven surface an enigma to my townie's feet — this is a road in name only.

'The light is barely enough to show me the way, yet there is a curious glow about everything, as though the moon shines full upon the cloud cover. But there is no moon beyond that dripping blanket; no source there for the orange light that illuminates the rank, overgrown fields either side of the climbing way.

I continue, the gas can I carry another unaccustomed burden, one that flattens my soles in the rills cascading down the hill. Every step forward is a partial slip that makes me painfully aware of my years.

I pause for breath, looking up towards my goal - my new home. Here too, the orange glimmer that might be some luminous quality of the October rushgrass delineates the low cottage, a silhouette, darkest against the dark sky.

My heart thuds in my chest more evenly now, and I practise a few more steps beneath my load, each a new experience in pain. And I thought cycling up Bigyn Hill could hurt! The water flowing past my feet picks up the light and becomes molten copper... Is my fatigue affecting my sight ?

I peer over the wire rims of my spectacles — the lenses are a confusion of raindrops — and there is the origin of that mystic glow. The windows that guide me are rich, warm beacons of candlelight incredibly brilliant despite the simple nature of the source. As warm as the love I know awaits me.

A few short weeks ago my return from shopping trips to Tesco would be greeted by five small figures eager to unload the box I had fitted to the back of the big trike. I thought I was fit, propelling that ungainly contraption up the last hill to the house.

Now I wonder at it and at the new life we have chosen.

Blown in on the wind and far from home ...

Home?

I stand wobbling beneath the cold, wet, steel cylinder and the ridiculously heavy vapour it contains and contemplate the scene before me. From council house to this — from every convenience to none. Not even a road.

I uproot my feet and step out towards those beckoning windows. When the door opens there will be a rush of warm air that will fog my glasses. I will barely see the hands that reach out to help me, take my load and wipe my dripping waterproofs. But in the darkness of that muddy path is one fact I can see clearly for all my twilight myopia and stinging eyes: there is no thing better than this ...

No thing better.

Rose

*D*eliberately he set the bottle in the centre of the table. He placed the glass equidistant between the bottle and the edge.

He fetched a chair and stood it opposite the glass.

He sat with both hands upon his knees. He stared at the glass, hesitating — was this really the best course?

He fumbled in his jacket pocket, withdrew the bottle of pills and studied it critically. They had been sitting in the bathroom cabinet for nearly twenty years. Why? For this special destiny?

> TUINAL
>
> One capsule to be taken before bed
>
> Do not exceed stated dose
>
> Keep medicines away from children
>
> 1-8-76

He put the bottle next to the glass and sat once more, staring at the arrangement.

At least, he thought, I might as well have a drink and give the matter some consideration.

He poured a moderate amount of whiskey into the glass, carefully capped the bottle and set it back in its place.

He took a sip. Pulled a face as he swallowed — as he always did on the first one. He used to remark on it.

For the first time he noticed the tablecloth. It was of light creamy colour with a sinuous border of wild rose. In the centre was an ellipse of similar design though less sinuous, more intertwined. It looked like a thicket guarding the bottle which stood in its centre.

The pill bottle stood picket betwixt glass and enclosure. He adjusted

164

its position slightly to get the line straight, then sighted along the row, an action that took his eye beyond to the wallpaper ...

She had always liked roses.

There were roses in the bathroom, on the tiles above the bath ...

'Rose by name and Rose by nature,' she would say. Oh, but she was a thorny one.

Another sip, a swallow. An empty glass.

He took the whiskey from its safe retreat and refilled the glass. Drink this one, then sample a pill, he decided ... may. Once more he drank, swiftly becoming light-headed; it was some time since he had eaten.

Something on the tablecloth moved. The border had begun to undulate, moving left to right.

'Bloody roses,' he muttered aloud. 'Everywhere, bloody roses!' Well, there was blood enough now, he concluded in silence.

She was Beauty and the Beast in one.

He opened the Tuinal bottle and made to tip one capsule from it — but now he was clumsy and several tumbled clear, red and blue bullets rolling on the tablecloth.

Russian Roulette, he thought. He could pop one to try with the next sip ...

... he did. And spluttered half the mouthful up into his nasal passage where it stung unpleasantly. But the capsule had gone down.

Mildly surprised that nothing was happening, he swallowed another — then a third.

The glass was empty and the bottle seemed a long way off all of a sudden. He had to rest his arms on the table to reach for it.

He paused with his hands both gripping the bottle. Did he really need to do this? There was money in the bank and a passport in his desk. He could get clean away ... it wasn't too late ... he could walk off the effects if he went now. Strong black coffee ... make himself sick ...

He was really dizzy now and a bit frightened ... a lot frightened. He did not really want to go into this sweaty miasma of fumes. He had forgotten how he hated feeling drunk.

With a great effort, he pushed the bottle away, his forearms crushing the errant capsules as he fought to get his legs under him.

Something was preventing him — something sharp!

The wild rose twined around his torso, up about his arms, pinioning him to the chair.

Desperately he thrashed his limbs to free himself, a rather unco-ordinated effort as the alcohol, diluted, transmuted the barbiturate.

It's not enough to kill, some corner of his mind told him in lucid syllables … he'd sleep it off …

He managed to throw himself backwards, turning over the chair, the table, bringing down the cloth across his face …

The scent of rose was strong — stronger than the whiskey.

The briar was strong, unrelenting. It would not let him go.

She would not let him go.

Aileni C Noyle
Inishfree Writers

The Hard Man

The Hard Man sat at the end of the bar counting his teeth with his tongue.

He stared absently at his sepia reflection in the Guinness Toucan mirror, the drink in front of him an hour old. Nineteen — no, twenty.

They felt strong and deeply rooted, except for that one near the back at the top. He worried it with his searching tongue, waggling it about until it rewarded him with a sharp pang. It would have to come out soon. Maybe if he waited long enough, somebody would oblige him.

That's where the others had gone...

Amazingly the front ones were still there.

He took great care of his teeth. Not only because he thought that a man's natural teeth should be preserved. It was just that they were part of his arsenal. Like his fists and feet, and head and knees and elbows and fingers. And something else. He lifted his glass and took a thoughtful sip. Ritchie O'Donnel. Wee Ritchie.

Choking to death before anyone knew he was dying, false teeth jammed down his throat by a hard, black fist in a rat-hole bar in Morocco.

He had carried him back to the boat and handed his body over to the ship's doctor. Then he went back to the bar and found the man who had killed him.

He looked down at his hands.

How many teeth had they extracted from unwilling jaws?

'You okay there, mister?'

He looked up to see the aproned figure of the barman wiping wet rings off the bar-top in sweeping semi-circles.

He liked it here. The quiet conviviality of the place. Dark corners, sociable shadows.

He glanced at the clock over the bar. Early yet. Raised his glass and drained it. Have one more, then ... what? God, he missed the wee man's company. He cocked his chin at the empty glass.

He watched the barman pull the pint, holding the glass at just the right angle, twisting it this way and that, nursing the froth into the famous head. Then he seemed to abandon it to tend to other things while the smooth cream crawled up the glass, but, just when it was sure to overflow, he turned fluidly, knowing exactly how long these things took, flipped back the lever, skimmed the bulging head. The pint was delivered, bar wiped.

The Hard Man took a sip, sieving the dark stout through the foaming crown.

For the next half hour, he sat as unobtrusively as his size allowed and watched the place come to life.

Saturday night in Toner's Bar was an unpredictable affair for one reason only, but at least you were sure of a good pint. And to the men who frequented the establishment this was of vital importance, for not all pints are created equal.

See, it was all in the way it was pulled.

You breasted up to the bar, caught his eye, gave your order and watched Harry work.

He pushes the big Guinness glass underneath the gleaming brass tap and pulls on the black-handled lever. Circles the glass, tipping it left and right, bringing it down gradually to rest on the drain. Turns away. Thick, creamy foam drizzles silently into the glass, climbing slowly up the sides, the yellowy-white suds swirling in a miniature sandstorm, gradually clearing to reveal the strong, dark nectar at the bottom. Meantime, Harry grabs three bottles of Red Heart stout between the fingers of his right hand, three shorts glasses in his left, pushes the chunky glasses, one at a time, up against the Powers Whiskey optic and lets it measure out the usual quarter of a gill, this while he's opening the stout bottles on the opener nailed to the table top. Not a drop spilled.

All the while the pint glass is slowly filling.

Puts the whiskies and the bottles of stout on the bar and from underneath takes three thin glasses which join the bottles of stout. Turns to the till.

'That'll be —' telling you the debt. You hand your money over.

The pint glass is three quarters full and rising...

Rings the money into the till, extracts the change, spins on his heel.

...creamy head lapping at the rim of the glass, sandstorm boiling underneath, turning to black below...

'Your change —' Smacks it onto the bar.

...foaming lather oozing its way above the rim, one edge beginning to droop into a rivulet, ready to roll down the side.

168

Casually pushes back the tap lever, cutting off the flow, scoops the glass clear. Black as velvet with an inch-wide, thick, perfect, creamy head.

Thirsty? Damn right.

'—and your Guinness.' Palms whack the bar top, gaze sweeping left to right along the bar. *Wipe.* 'Next...?'

Holy Flip came in, water dripping from his nose, coat front dark from the pelting rain. He clapped his hands together and rubbed them to and fro, then rolled them over each other, washing them. He took off his rain-spattered glasses and wiped them with his handkerchief, squinting like a mole around the room.

'S' bucketin' out there,' he said to nobody.

He shuffled to the bar, shrugging his scrawny shoulders quickly several times, sucking through pursed lips.

'Gis a pint, Harry.'

'Hiya Flip.' Harry was already working the lever, pouring the first of the two pints that was Flip's limit. Flip waited and watched.

'The boys in?'

'Davy and Willy're in the snug. Sam's not in yet.'

Flip looked around furtively, voice dropping a conspiratorial octave

'What about ah — yer man?'

'No sign of him — yet.'

'Aye, well, we can but hope.' Flip wandered off to join 'the boys'.

Harry went down the bar, back to the discussion he had left to serve Flip. He stood absently drying glasses while the three men in front of the bar debated the proper way to pronounce 'Mexico'.

'Listen, the Mexicans call it *Meheeco*. Y'hear it all the time in the cowboy films. *Old Meheeco* th' call it.'

'I think it's *Meckico*. Like a sort of a kay.'

'And I'm tellin' ye, it's *Mexico*. Don't they sing it in that song? 'South of the Border down Mex—'

'Nah — it's *Meheeco*, the axe sounds like — aye, like a haitch — that's the proper way to say it.'

'Ach your arse! You mean I'm gonna have to get a *tahi*-cab to take me home th' night!'

Roars of laughter from all three. Harry joined in, enjoying the old joke.

His establishment was situated half a mile or so from Belfast's Pollock dock. Had its own regulars lived near, but got the usual hotchpotch of sailors and dockers. The sign was uninspiring but it said enough.

'TONER'S BAR'

in blue and gold lettering over the front window.

'H. Toner (Prop.) '

in smaller letters underneath.

Inside the decor was utilitarian. Brown panelled snugs in the corners, tables and chairs in the middle, the odd stool at the long bar. No upholstery here, was a man's pub. It reeked of that mixture of stout and whiskey and stale cigarette smoke that clogs the pores of every brick and plank in places like this, where working men gather to drink.

'Sorry I'm late Harry...'

Harry smiled at the whisper. Caught again. He turned to face the man behind him.

'S'alright, Ghosty,' he said, 'Not too busy anyway. Just give the floor a wee lick and tidy the tables.'

The legacy of a lifetime of indoor pursuits, Arthur McGuigan's pasty white pallor was strictly preserved from the rays of the sun by the checked cloth cap and ancient grey dexter, worn summer and winter. He was thin as the handle on his brush. Rolled his own cigarettes — awful, throat-searing tobacco clumsily fumbled into a miserable stick of a fag which sat in the middle of his thin lips and refused to stay lit. Spent more on matches than he did on tobacco.

Ghosty didn't meet people. Sort of just — appeared to them.

He slipped silently into the back room behind the bar and emerged with his brush.

'Is the Bully...?'

Harry shook his head. 'Nah, Ghosty, not yet.'

'Mebbe he'll give us a miss,' whispered The Ghost.

'Aye, mebbe,' Harry said.

He came in bang on eight o'clock. Descended. Like a bucket of cold water.

Voices dipped, shoulders drooped. Heads turned to look and quickly turned away.

And as always the scrape of chairs as the faint-hearted headed for the door.

The Bully sat down, usual place.

'Pint 'na half 'un!!' Voice like a damn foghorn.

Harry saw him but thought. Frig him! He can wait. He was fixing a hot scotch for Jim Rafferty's cold, sugar first, then the cloves. Lemon,

Jim? Jim shook his head then glanced down the bar and said Oops! Harry whirled round in time to see a pint glass exploding in shards on the floor behind the bar.

'*Pint 'na half 'un!!*'

Harry came flying down the bar, red-faced and furious.

'What the hell's gates do you think you're—?'

'Pint 'na half 'un!'

'I'm serving somebody, for Jesus sake — I'll be with you in a m—.'

The Bully reached sideways, grabbed the half-finished pint from the hand of the man sitting next to him and hurled it at the wall behind the bar, where it burst amid a spray of foaming stout.

'Pint 'na HALF 'UN!!' he roared.

Harry could see the situation getting out of control.

'Alright — *alright!* For Chrissake! Pint and a half 'un — *pint and a half 'un!*'

He called to Ghosty to clean the mess behind the bar, but Ghosty was already there with his brush. Harry crunched through the debris and grabbed a whiskey glass.

'If your Da was alive—' he began to say.

'Leave my Da out of it, wee man, or I'll wreck the friggin' place!!'

Jesus Christ! And him just in through the door. Harry Toner backed off, hating the bastard. Hating himself too.

The mood of the place had changed, as it always did when The Bully came in. Sat next to the GENTS, on his usual stool at the bar, smoking continuously, stubbing them out with his foot on the floor. Harry Toner fetched the whiskey and poured the pint. Gathered the thrown coins. By the time he handed over the change, the whiskey had already disappeared down the man's cavernous gullet, Guinness following it. Head thrown back, mouth agape, the dark liquid sloshed down the gulping thrapple. Thump! Empty glass whacks down on the bar, creamy tide of froth slithering down the sides.

'Same again, wee man.'

Was Flip's bladder landed him in trouble. That or he was drinking too fast and it had gone to his head. Whatever it was, he committed the cardinal sin of going to the toilet and realised his mistake as he passed the hunched figure of the Bully, but by then…

The gorilla-like hand shot out and Flip's scrawny arm was clutched in a blood-stopping grip. The little man was jerked off balance and hauled unceremoniously to the bar. The thigh-thick arm circled his shoulder, drew him in, knocking the wind out of him. Bully growling.

'Sing us a song, wee man!' The way a bear would, if bears took drink.

Flip's face was crimson as he tried to draw breath. Gagging.

'C—can't...breathe...'

'What? C'mon, frig ye, *c'mon?*' roared the Bully. Holy Flip wheezed, face purpling.

The Bully began to sing, rocking from side to side, crushing the little man in a one-armed vice.

'*A muth-er's luv's a blessin'*....' whacking his glass on the bar in time to the song. '*Wher-ivver yoo-ooh may roam* — sing up, c'mon, damn ye!'

Harry Toner took one look at Flip's distressed face and charged down the bar.

'For Chrissake Bully, you're chokin' him.'

'*Don't fer-git your Muth-errr...*' Crushing the skinny shoulders tighter.

Harry reached across the bar, tried to disengage the stranglehold. The Bully's right hand flew out and grabbed him by the throat.

'Stay out of it, wee man.'

It was the first time The Bully had ever laid a finger on him, and the strength of him was terrifying. He pushed, and Harry windmilled back against the shelves. But the awful grip lessened on Flip and Harry saw that he was catching his breath again.

'You alright, Flip?'

Flip nodded, waving his hand, still unable to speak. Face blue.

'Let him breathe, for God's sake.' Harry stood a respectful distance from that crushing paw. He saw Davy and Sam hovering nearby, wanting to help but just as shit-scared as he was.

'He can't breathe, dammit!'

The Bully let go of Holy Flip.

'Ah, go on, frig off, you wheezy oul' shite.'

With a vicious sideways swipe, he brought his arm across the wee man's chest and sent him sprawling backwards. Flip hit the wall with his back and his legs buckled. He slid down on his backside to the floor. Davy and Sam made to go to his aid but Flip waved them away. He rose slowly, looking at the Bully's back. Then he shuffled into the toilet.

'There's no doubt, big lad —,' Harry said. '— you can certainly handle nine-stone asthmatics.'

'Pint 'na half 'un!!' said The Bully.

Harry saw John Clancy come in and looked at the clock. Quarter-past nine.

Like a damned cuckoo. Every night, same time. He knew what John drank but made no move to get it. Just wanted to hear John order it.

Turned his back to the bar. Heard the rap of knuckles on the bar-top.

'Innkeeper!' (*It was Mr Macawber*) 'I wish to purchase several measures of ale for quaffing purposes. Please be kind enough to make yourself available for the vending of same.'

Harry turned, grinning. Loved this.

'What're y'having, John?' knowing anyway.

'A flagon of your finest for the thrapple and a small low-flyer for the chill.'

Harry pulled the pint of Guinness and while it was drizzling into the glass he poured a measure of Grouse whiskey into a small tumbler. He skimmed the head of the pint, brought both drinks to the end of the bar. Clancy looked with relish at the creamy stout.

'What sort of fee is attached to this transaction?'

Harry told him.

Clancy gave him a fiver. 'Accept this remuneration,' he said grandly. Harry grinned and shook his head, taking the money and getting the change from the till. He brought it back and smacked it down on the bar-top. Clancy had the pint to his head, drank about a third of it and set it down slowly on the bar. He lifted the tumbler of whiskey in salute.

'Your health, landlord, and that of your offspring.' Knocking it back with theatrical flourish. He set the empty glass down onto the counter and smacked his lips. Then he turned and surveyed the bar.

'S'quiet tonight, Harry.' Sounding quite normal and un-Macawber.

'Aye, and I hope it stays like that.' Harry rolled his eyes to where the Bully sat glowering round the room. 'So, John, what are you up to these days? Working still?'

'Ach, well, I had that job in the store of the brewery, as you know. Handy enough, loading the vans and that.' He patted his pockets for cigarettes, lit one and said round the smoke. 'Coupla weeks ago the manager asked me if I would fancy a job stocktaking. Bit more responsibility, more money too. Happy days, right? So I starts stocktaking on the Wednesday—' he took a long gulp and drained his glass. '— and got the boot on the Friday.'

'What? Yer kiddin'. Why?'

'Was takin' too much of it.'

Harry burst into laughter while Clancy blew smoke at the ceiling. 'That's what you get for enjoyin' your work, Clance. What'd you drink.'

Enter Macawber.

'A mere trifle. A bagatelle. A paltry crate of Alec, perhaps a duo of same.'

173

'And you were caught?'

'With the red mitt.'

'And...?'

'The rascals informed the constabulary. I appear before the assizes on the morrow.'

'What, for two crates of Guinness?' Harry turned his head to the side and lowered his voice. 'I wish that bastard would appear before the assizes.' Telling John about the business with Holy Flip. John's face darkened and he glanced down the bar at the giant.

'In truth,' said *Macawber*. 'the scoundrel is spoiled for want of a sound thrashing.'

He fished in his pocket and produced a ten pound note.

'But enough of the unwashed rabble. Fetch copious amounts of ale, stout fellow, and partake of one yourself.'

Harry fetched the drinks, said cheers John, and watched the little alcoholic thread his way to join Flip & Co. It was half-past nine.

His sixth pint was halfway down the glass.

The Bully began to rock on his stool. He sucked his teeth and smacked his lips, glaring moodily around the room. Nobody sat within twenty feet of him. *Snobby bastards.*

The floor around him was littered as usual with squashed cigarette ends.

Across the bar, the gliding form of Ghosty McGuigan flitted in and out between the tables, studiously steering his brush around the already clean floor. He spotted the pile of debris beneath The Bully's seat and moved on silent, plimsolled feet. His brush shooshed into the scattered butts. Nudged the leg of the stool.

'Excuse me...' whispered The Ghost.

The Bully's head swivelled round at the unexpected arrival.

'What the f—?'

He put one foot on the floor and with the other he trapped the head of the brush. Ghosty looked up at The Bully. The Bully turned to Ghosty.

Without a word of warning he bunched one sausage-fingered fist and hit him savagely in the middle of the face.

Ghosty's nose exploded in a scarlet spray and he collapsed backward to the floor, out like a light, his cap skittering across the room and fetching up against the front door. He lay stretched out like a corpse for burial, arms neatly at his sides, mouth wide open and pouring blood.

Two of his front teeth were broken. The skinny fag was squashed into his shattered lips.

The whole bar was stunned into slack-jawed silence, staring in disbelief at the still form of Ghosty McGuigan.

Harry Toner came tearing out from behind the bar carrying towels and a basin of water.

'Jesus God, Bully, there was no call for that!' He was livid with revulsion and anger.

'He's a creepy bastard.' The Bully turned casually back to the bar and lifted his pint.

'He deserved it!'

People crowded round to help. Harry carefully bathed the bloodied face of The Ghost, fishing in his mouth for the broken teeth, wincing when he saw the extent of the damage. He gently turned him over on his side to prevent him choking. Ghosty moaned.

Somebody rang for an ambulance and Ghosty, now conscious but unaware of what had happened, was carted off to the Royal. Somebody went to tell his 'Mammy'.

Eventually the place settled. But the incident took its effect on the rest of the patrons of Toner's Bar. The waves of loathing and disgust which swept through the pub cleared it of all but the most hardy drinkers.

And here was Harry Toner (*prop*), at just past ten on a Saturday night, presiding over a hushed, almost empty establishment, which should have been packed to the doors with talking, laughing, back-slapping drinkers. He looked at the massive form of the instigator of this situation, hunched over his pint, wreathed in smoke, indifferent to the muted atmosphere around him. Big fish in a wee pond.

If I was twenty years younger…

Aye, and ten stone heavier and twelve inches taller and had the balls. Who you kiddin' Harry?

'You're a bad, bad bastard, Willy McCann,' he said bitterly.

But he said it to himself.

Out of the corner of his eye he caught a movement at the other end of the bar.

The Hard Man had watched the incident impassively enough. He'd seen worse, in many places. Was none of his business. He caught the barman's attention with an upward lift of his chin. Harry came down the bar.

'Yessir,' he said.

The man said same again and Harry scooped the empty glass away.

175

'Where's the GENTS?'

Harry nodded over his right shoulder. Bottom of the bar, turn right. He heard the whack of the empty glass on the bar-top.

'Pint 'n' half 'un!' roared the Bully.

'—and watch yourself,' said Harry.

The Hard Man stopped halfway out of his seat. 'Why?' he said. Then he headed down the bar.

Harry Toner felt the hairs on the back of his neck prickle upright as he watched the tall man walk casually down the room. He began to wipe the top of the bar, sidling to the right, down towards the corner, where The Bully was sitting.

The Bully looked up as The Hard Man approached. His piggy eyes appraised him.

The Hard Man strode slowly by, looking straight ahead while the Bully swivelled in his seat to follow him, like a camera tracking an actor, spiteful eyes boring into his back as he went through the door marked 'GENTLEMEN'. Bully got up off the stool.

The room fell still. Tense as a hawser. Then low murmurs of expectancy began to flit among the tables. Harry Toner quietly lifted the flap and slipped out from behind the bar.

The Bully glared at the toilet door.

The voices rhubarbed louder.

The door of the GENTS opened.

Glasses stopped midway to mouths.

The noise drained away.

The Bully had positioned himself right in front of the door, legs braced, arms folded across his chest. When The Hard Man emerged he found his way blocked by twenty-two stone of beef and bad temper. He stood and waited, knowing what would happen next.

'You're havin' a drink!'

'No,' said The Hard Man, quiet as you like. Harry Toner clenched his fists in fervent supplication. *Go on Bully, do your stuff—be yourself...*

The Bully obliged, loud as a foghorn.

'What's wrong — my company not **good enough**?'

'That's right —' The Hard Man's face relaxed, his eyes cooled and he prepared himself, choosing the insult meticulously.

'— I prefer to drink — with men.'

The softly-spoken words roared at the silence. Harry Toner felt Flip's hand on his arm.

'Holy flip, Harry, they're gonna wreck the place on ye!'

'It's alright, Flip, it's insured,' Harry said calmly, slipping the 'OUT

OF ORDER' notice over the public phone. He then walked casually to the front door and locked it as The Bully kicked away the stool and launched himself at The Hard Man...

...found him gone, and whirled round, straight into a lethally curving right-hander that caught him square on the side of the face. The crack of his breaking jaw was like a whip in the silence.

He shook his bear-like head to clear it, then with creditable agility caught the Hard man on the chin with a whistling roundhouse and was in turn hit three times in rapid succession by a granite fist. The trip-hammer blows rained on his nose, splitting it to the bone. Blood fountained out of the gaping wound.

He said *ahhhh* and lost four teeth as bunched knuckles bludgeoned him straight in the face. His roar of pain and fury was choked by a slicing left hook which opened his lip like a fish's mouth.

'G-gl-l-a-arrgg..,' he spluttered and spun round like a Spanish bull, sprinkling a ring of red polka dots around the floor. The Hard Man hit him again across the temple. His eyebrow burst open.

The Bully staggered ponderously around the room, knocking aside tables and chairs, scattering bottles, smashing glasses, arms flailing uselessly at his remorseless assailant who, silently and coldly, got down to the business he did best.

It was a cruel, savage beating, frightening in its calm brutality, awesome in its violent serenity.

The patrons of Toner's Bar watched in total silence as perfect, poetic justice was served on Bully McCann, and there wasn't a man who didn't will and propel each crashing blow with his own clenched fists and eagerly nodding head and not a one didn't count it a privilege to be there. With his back to the locked front door, Harry Toner watched grimly, face flat and expressionless. Inside he was cheering like a hooligan.

It was over in less than five minutes. Bully McCann folded his knees and finally hit the deck amid a crescendo of tinkling glass and splintering wood. His face was a swollen porridge of purple and red, hiding the ruined jaw, and later doctors would discover ten smashed ribs.

For a minute The Hard Man stood looking down at the prostrate body. He spat delicately and a red-rooted tooth landed on the Bully's chest. Slowly he lifted his head and looked around the room. Open-mouthed men stared back at him. His only enemy lay at his feet.

The pub was paralysed as the magnitude of what had happened began to sink in.

Then the shock yielded to a rising hubbub of amazement. The

owner of the establishment tore his eyes away from the bleeding wreck on the floor. Searched for words. Jesus.

'Ah—would you like a drink, mister—?' Harry Toner's mouth was dry, needing one himself. '—on the house.'

The Hard Man turned to him. 'Salt water.'

'What?'

He held up a raw-knuckled fist.

'Follow me.' Harry led the way behind the bar and into the back room, stemming the flood of questions he desperately wanted to ask and left The Hard Man dabbing his bleeding knuckles with the warm, salty water. He went out into the bar. Men were crowding around the unconscious hulk of The Bully, their rhubarb-rhubarb of talk incredulous, punctuated with the disbelieving shaking of heads.

'Did'ya ever see the like o' that in yer whole life?'

'Was that some scrap or what?'

'Aye, picked on the wrong fella…'

'…finally got what he deserved, the vicious bas—'

'Indeed, sir. The scoundrel was roundly trounced, of a surety.'

Harry gave it five minutes then cleared a space around the injured man. He told Flip to call an ambulance.

'But the phone's out of order, Harry.'

'It's alright, Flip. Take the notice off, that'll fix it.'

'Are you gonna tell the cops?' somebody asked. The whole bar rounded him.

'Tell them what?' said Harry.

'About ah — about the ah— fight.' The man muttered, cursing his own big mouth.

Harry slushed the mop through a pool of blood.

'What fight?' he said.

Harry Toner made Bully McCann as comfortable as he could while he waited for the ambulance to arrive. How many times had he done this for the victims of the man on the floor? He knew one thing, though. The Bully would never be back. The real world had finally caught him up. *The little pond had leaked and let in a bigger fish.*

Christ! He thought of the tall man in the back room. He'd buy him that drink now. *Drink? Ten* drinks! A *barrel* o' the stuff for Jazus' sake!

He crunched his way through the shards of broken glass and into the room behind the bar. The basin of cooling water was on the table, stained a pale pink, the cloth folded neatly beside it. The back door was flapping open, letting in the gusting Saturday night rain.

The chair was empty. So was the room.

178

'Give us a pint?'

Harry turned round to find Holy Flip looking at him over the bar.

'What's this, Flip, a *third* one?'

'That fight sobered me up again,' said Flip, like he'd just decked The Bully himself

Harry drew the pint and set it in front of the little man, then poured himself a generous measure of Black Bush whiskey. He pushed the offered coins back across the bar.

'S'alright, Flip,' he smiled. 'Tonight —' raising his glass, '— this one's on the house.'

Their glasses clinked together as the *nah-nah-nah-nah* of an ambulance swelled in the street outside.

'Cheers Flip,' said Harry Toner.

'Well, holy flip!' said Holy Flip

Gerry McAuley
Newtownabbey Writers' Group

Geduld

Wenn ich auch weiß
um die unsagbare
    Blütenpracht,
wenn ich auch ahne
den allumfassenden Duft
und im Geiste all dies
als wunderbares Ganzes vor
    mir sehe
und alles in mir drängt
es jetzt und gleich zu sehen,
so muß ich doch warten
bis nach und nach
in unendlicher Gesetzmäßgkeit
die Pflanze sich entwickelt.
Und erst die frühen Sprossen,
dann das Blatt
und eins ums andere sich
    entfaltet.
Und micn freuen
an ledem Schritt,
weiß ich doch
urn dieses Wunder.

Patience

Although I know
of the inexpressible luxuriance
    of blossoms,
although I anticipate
the universal smell
and in mind all this
I can see before me as
    wonderful Whole
and all in me urges
to see it now and at once,
Yet I have to wait
until little by little,
according to never-ending law
the plant is being formed.
And first the early sprouts,
then the leaf
and one by one is unfolding.

And I'm delighted
by each step
since I know
about this miracle!

Heidi Schulz
Inishfree Writers

Inishfreeing

1.

Speaking in suburban tones
edged by a sea of troubles
factories and jam jars conspire,
a collection of clones.
Precisely cropped hedges and thought
a reformed occupation,
always the need to seek fresh pheromones.

2.

The hard nosed core
spits out her children
upon rivers of love and hate,
rippling a red handed velour
that never quite sleeps.
Picking up light instead of darkness
on a procrastinating shore.

3.

Another sea bites imagination,
a brown skinned camp
wigwam's drying across a bog.
The gate post collie, a near collision,
gossamer wires gleamed from pole to pole
joining the World Wide Web,
around every corner a mountainous exhilaration.

4.

The great escapement
within a clock of illumination
mountain sun dial shows the hour,

a silent sacrament.
The bungalow stands in emptiness
but turns no one away,
a special kind of fulfilment.

5.

Ropes made of gravity and magnitude
held a lolling summer star
on a marbled eider up or down,
checking the longitude.
Islands transmit a natural magnetism
tuning into the right wavelength,
reception of a holy quietude.

6.

People talk in a glissando
words fall upon words
as waves fall into waves.
The moth reaches beyond the imago
crimson conversations from flower to flower,
spiders in my hair mean good fortune
island to island an intermezzo.

7.

Across the sound on Arranmore
a confetti of homesteads drift,
on Inishfree an ocean calls
flight from poverty a hard chore
a continent replies.
Cursive style echoed the carrier wave
feelings of the heart sore.

8.

Old stories found in an attic
the hunger for new world news
fishermen stroke the silver scaled darlings.
Letter lines that crisscross the pelagic
a vengeful father chooses his time
to net his human souls,
a sense of the tragic.

9.

Soundings in fathoms
four hundred years later
the house still sets sail,
on an island that gently hums.
Gaze catches gaze
great grandmother's, and father's hang on
faintly smiling phantoms.

10.

Hands of rain play a pibroch
through ruined rooms,
uncomfortable furniture
stuffed by a century's flock.
Clown of time
tells threadbare jokes
across lough and lough.

11.

No question of identity
the music of place
easy on a Dal Riada ear,
nature's subtle sorcery.
Children whistle on the tra
calling up departed spirits
reaffirming ancestry.

12.

Clinker boats linger
find a true compass
on a low August tide.
Atlantic singer
breathes in and out correctly
appreciates the northern lights,
the earth's magnetic whisper.

13.

Stone is an excellent raconteur
rain has a good vocabulary
discovers every crack and flaw.

The ocean not known for being demure
wears away things,
muscle, bone, and mind, take a stand,
memory makes a strong armature.

14.

Expectation of different weather
leaving the homes of Dún na nGal,
caught red handed bathing
in the rowan trees' blushing river.
Stony lands revealed kind hearts,
a daddy-longlegs on clouded glass
the past and future quiver.

15.

The close relation
a charm of goldfinches
pinking prayer over a Protestant graveyard,
found a lean congregation.
The smattering of headstones
shows a sense of belonging,
an old and new confabulation.

16.

Fibres intertwine playfully
Antrim linen and Donegal tweed
establish a colourful weave,
issue a joyous plea.
Strangers leave a residue
building an archive of friendship,
the electrification of Inishfree.

Iain Campbell Webb
Newtownabbey Writers' Group

Winter Midpoint

At this midpoint of winter
When days are short
And nights stretch into endless hours
Of dark and solitude,
I look back to the summer sun
Remembering
And forward to the springtime
Come — again.

The precious daylight hours are filled
With joyous observations,
Little things.
The wagtail bobbing by the door
For crumbs,
The cattle huddled in a bunch
For warmth,
Tiny mussels growing on the rocks
In clusters,
A promise of the new that is to come.

And the sea washes constantly
Whirling and swirling
Slowly eroding
Smoothing and moulding
Wishing and sighing.

Night-time stretches endlessly till dawn.
Candlelight is soft upon the eye.
The turf glows warmly on the fire
And sleep comes easily.

Mrs Noah

1

Why is there a giraffe in my kitchen, Noah?
Says Mrs Noah to him.
The Lord says gather two of each kind.
The Lord says do it for Him

Well that's alright, says Mrs Noah,
If the Lord says, then it's grand.
I can cope with a giraffe in my kitchen, Noah,
As long as you give me a hand.

2

What are you doing with all that wood?
Says Mrs Noah to him.
I'm building a boat for the Lord, says Noah.
I'm building a boat for Him.

Well that's alright, says Mrs Noah,
If the Lord says, then that's clear.
You can build your boat, says Mrs Noah,
But just don't build it in here!

3

Did you ever see such rain, Noah?
Said Mrs Noah to him.
The Lord said He would make it rain.
Well that, I think, is grim.

It's going to rain for forty days.
Noah looked at the sky.
But that's not fair, said Mrs Noah.
I can't get my washing dry.

4

There's water up to the windows, Noah
Said Mrs Noah to him.
Time to get on board, says Noah.
And God then shut them in.

The water rose and went on rising.
Said Mrs Noah to him,
How long will it last? I don't know, dearest,
But God will keep us fast.

5

Why did He choose you, Mr Noah?
Said Mrs Noah to him.
Because I'm good, apparently
Said Mr Noah to she.

Well, that's quite right, and as it should be
Said Mrs Noah to him.
But what about me? said Mrs Noah.
Why am I here? said she.

6

Because I love you and need you here,
Said Mr Noah to she.
Oh — well that's alright, says Mrs Noah
Very quietly.

7

I'm trying to get your tea, Noah,
Well thank you, dear, said he,
But there's an elephant in the cupboard, Noah.
Well, best invite him for tea.

But the mice have been in the bread, Noah.
Well never mind, said he,
We'll have some cheese and potatoes and peas.
Well, if you're sure, said she.

8

Noah, there's nothing left to see.
But Noah already knew.
The flowers, the rivers, the mountains high
Had disappeared from view.

What will become of us now, Noah?
Said Mrs Noah to him.
The water has covered it all, Noah.
Oh what are we going to do?

9

And the Ark it floated upon the sea
One hundred and fifty days
With nothing to see but sea each day,
No creatures, no people, no sight of land,
Until one day a breeze did blow
And the rain it ceased and the waters eased
And Noah raised a dove in his hand.
Go forth, my friend, and look for land.

10

And the waters abated off the earth
And the dove returned to him
Bringing a leaf from an olive branch,
Bringing it back for him.

The Ark it rested on Ararat
On top of the mountain high
And the waters drained from off the land
Until it was nice and dry.

11
Take your animals, two by two
The Lord said unto Noah.
Go you hence and multiply
The Lord God said to him.

They stepped outside and looked around,
Mrs Noah and him.
A brand new world, a bright new day.
Let's make a new start, says Mr Noah.
Yes, let's, says Mrs to him.

Angela Morrey
Inishfree Writers

Memory Poem

(for Karen)

This is the day I heard your voice again
and saw your face in the shadows.
The rain wept bitterly
in the darknesses in your eyes;
your hair black as sloe,
your hands like aloeswood,
as aromatic as the black earth
of Glas-na-cradan.
There I plucked you a wild, white rose
to braid into your hair,
its pale-pink stamens quivering in the wind.

The trees we met under are all cut down,
their stumps like gravestones
there in the moonlight.
There, in the moonlight, I saw them,
and I remembered you.

Jim Johnston
Newtownabbey Writers' Group

winter solstice

getting up

with the light

few days ago playing

games of 'Go' with a first

timer my friend getting annoyed at

the stones not connecting trying

to leave a space for the stones

to float free the emptiness of 'Go'

letting go

sometimes

it's handy

to know

when to let go

boat hook

round the ring

on the quay

i would have

been pulled in

half decker

surging away

from the slipway

in a rough sea!

barry edgar pilcher
inishfree writers' group

Good Karma
(for R.K.)

Belfast Lough is grey and silver
my yoga sun is yellow and gold
my heart is like an old mosaic
pieces adrift on the surface of time

Carnmoney Hill, a green escarpment
my yoga world a stilled upheaval
my muscles stretch along the gnomon
sundial-wise to the rising sun

Glas-na-bradan is stream and silver
my yoga glen is silent and calm
this song is like an old expression
minted anew for the pleasure of you

Jim Johnston
Newtownabbey Writers' Group

Trying to Connect You

*J*essica ran to answer the phone before it rang off. She had been bathing Catriona, and it took her a while to reach the phone. It was George. 'What about Ellen?' he said with no explanatory preamble. He knew that Jessica would understand that he was suggesting his sister as a suitable minder for Catriona; while they attended the college reunion in just over a week's time. 'She could come here for the weekend,' George continued, 'Catriona would be happier at home, anyway.' 'Yes,' agreed Jessica, 'that would be OK if she could manage it.' It may be that Jessica's concern was for the mothering ability of Ellen, who seemed too career-orientated to be concerned with domestic matters. However, George merely assumed that it was the availability of a suitable time-slot that Jessica referred to. 'This parents' evening will keep me tied up till late,' he said, 'could you call Ellen and ask her?' Jessica agreed somewhat reluctantly, but returned to Catriona in the bathroom when she put down the phone. She needed time to prepare herself for the call to Ellen.

It was not that Jessica disliked Ellen, on the contrary, they seemed to get on well on their infrequent encounters. It was more that Ellen was everything Jessica was not - an increasingly successful career woman, a single, free spirit who could holiday in exotic places, an enthusiastic consumer of cultural events ranging from classical concerts to strange art installations. Jessica always felt a mixture of envy and inferiority when she considered Ellen's hectic and cosmopolitan life in London. Stuck here in Beckleton, not remote, but inconveniently distant from cultural centres, with a husband and child to care for, Jessica was unable to participate in the world that Ellen frequented, and had to content herself with village friends and amateur dramatics.

Having settled Catriona in bed, Jessica steeled herself and rang Ellen's London flat.

Because she was rehearsing in her mind what she would say, she did not really notice how long the phone was ringing, but eventually a tentative voice answered. 'Ellen? This is Jessica,' she began, continuing, 'How are you?' There was a pause, possibly while Ellen recovered her equanimity, but more likely while she matched the name 'Jessica' with an acquaintance. It was certainly unusual for Jessica to be phoning her, and perhaps not surprising that Ellen had some difficulty placing her voice. 'Oh, Jessica,' she eventually said, having recognised the caller as her sister-in-law, 'I'm fine, how are things with you?' A note of concern in her voice told Jessica that Ellen feared that she would only phone if there was some seriously bad news of George's health. 'Oh, we're all fine here,' she said to set Ellen's mind at rest. 'George is tied up at a parents' evening,' she continued, 'I'm phoning to see if you might be able to come up the weekend after next to look after Catriona while we're away at a college reunion.'

Jessica had not planned to ask quite so immediately. She had wanted to explain that they had made arrangements long ago before they had booked to go away and it was only Marjory's sudden illness that presented them with this last-minute problem. The last thing she wanted was for Ellen to think that she was disorganised. As usual, though, the conversation did not follow the path she envisaged, and she had found herself if asking the favour before she had really meant to. She could not know that the prospect of a weekend in the country seemed like a godsend to Ellen, who quickly agreed to the trip.

Jessica was relieved that things seemed to be settled so easily and was effusive in her thanks, feeling when she put the phone down that she had overdone it. Even if she had, Ellen did not notice. She was only too pleased to have an excuse to get away from London. Things were beginning to get her down. The pressure of work, the noise and the bustle of the city, but most of all those phone calls. Her cheery greeting would be met with silence. At first she assumed it was a wrong number or a fault on the line, but as they continued to occur she started to consider more sinister explanations. She imagined a shadowy male figure leering silently down the phone, or, worse still, with binoculars trained on the window of her flat. Angry and vituperative remarks on her part produced no response; she began to dread the phone ringing and her cheery greeting became decidedly diffident. Sometimes she refused to answer, as she almost had tonight, only relenting when the phone continued to ring.

It was arranged that George would meet Ellen at the nearest station where trains still stopped, and they exchanged pleasantries as they drove to Beckleton through the familiar Cotswold countryside. Ellen was always surprised at how pleasant it felt to be back, almost as though she was being comforted in the breast-like contours of the land.

The nostalgic glow increased as they reached the tawny stone houses of Beckleton and finally drew up at George's home, the house where they had both grown up. 'You're lucky to be able to live here,' said Ellen as the car stopped, 'this house has such good memories.' 'Yes,' replied George, 'I don't think I'd want to live anywhere else.' He rarely thought about it, it was just his home, where he had lived for most of his life, but when he did consider it, often as a result of someone else's comment, he realised that he was indeed fortunate.

Next morning Jessica showed Ellen around the kitchen and explained the routine. Ellen was once again impressed by the order in Jessica's affairs, with neat rows of home-made jams and pickles and cake-tins full of delicious looking home-made delicacies. The window-sills overflowed with luxuriant pot-plants which Ellen admired and was immediately offered. 'I'm running out of space,' said Jessica, 'I've more cuttings coming on in the conservatory.' Ellen felt decidedly lacking in feminine skills compared to this paragon of domesticity. Ellen's culinary endeavours were almost invariably disappointing, and house-plants wilted under her care. Catriona seemed to take after her mother, and obviously felt that she should be looking after Ellen, rather than the reverse. The contrast between Ellen's normal hectic life and the apparently peaceful existence in this welcoming old house was very marked, and Ellen felt a twinge of envy for Jessica's rural lifestyle. She enjoyed immersing herself in it all and rediscovering the half-forgotten joys of childhood, noting that being a little girl in Beckleton still seemed very much as she remembered it. When it came to reading a bedtime story she was delighted that Catriona selected a book that she remembered from her own childhood, containing stories of fairies painting flowers or decorating cobwebs with dewdrops.

When she had read one of the stories, to the evident delight of Catriona, the little girl looked at her seriously and asked 'Are there fairies in London?' 'Oh I think there must be, don't you?' replied Ellen, amused by the question . 'Well, where would they live, and what would they do?' asked Catriona. 'There are lots of parks with places for them to live,' said Ellen, 'and there are some flowers for them to paint, and cobwebs in the railings. I'm sure there's plenty for them to do.' This seemed to satisfy Catriona, who settled down in the bed, but as Ellen bent over to kiss her goodnight, Catriona looked up, and said, 'There's a place in our garden where the fairies live. I'll show you tomorrow if you like.' 'That would be nice,' said Ellen, walking to the door. 'See you in the morning.'

Next day Catriona kept her promise and led Ellen to a corner of the garden where a dilapidated stone shed stood. Behind it an overgrown hedge threw out blackthorn branches with honeysuckle interspersed among the thorns. 'This is a fairy thorn bush,' said Catriona proudly, 'the fairies live in there.' She indicated the gap between the shed and the hedge behind it. 'You won't see them because they're very shy,' she added, evidently repeating something she had been told. 'That's a nice secret place for them,' said Ellen, 'perhaps we'd better leave them in peace.' She led Catriona back to the lawn where they sat in the warm sunshine. 'Are there fairy thorn-bushes in London?' asked Catriona. 'I haven't seen any,' said Ellen truthfully. This seemed to worry Catriona, who obviously took a personal interest in the welfare of fairies. 'But the fairies need somewhere to live, else they can't do their magic,' said Catriona anxiously. She looked thoughtful and then asked Ellen, 'Have they asked you for somewhere to live?' 'How would they do that?' said Ellen. 'By magic somehow,' replied Catriona, 'they could magic a letter or a phone call.' Ellen immediately thought of her silent phone calls, and, rather to her surprise, found herself telling Catriona about them. 'I bet they're from the fairies,' said Catriona when she had heard Ellen's story, 'I bet they want somewhere to live.'

For the rest of their time together, Catriona and Ellen gathered things that would make a fairy home. Some of the house plants Ellen had been offered were selected, and small stones, mossy twigs and shards of pottery were collected from the garden and on their walks through the surrounding fields. They became increasingly conspiratorial, and agreed that the creation of this mini-dell would be their secret. Ellen was amused that Catriona seemed to regard herself as an expert on fairies, and the little girl gave her aunt detailed instructions on what fairies liked.

When George and Jessica returned they were pleased to see that a bond had formed between Catriona and Ellen, and were more than willing to part with the houseplants. Ellen was laden with extra bags of plants and knickknacks when they took her to the station, and George and Jessica were amused that Catriona had to whisper secretly to Ellen before she boarded the tram.

Once back in her fiat, Ellen arranged the mini-dell in the corner of the living room as best she could, and wrote a note to Catriona telling her about it. She also wrote to George and Jessica saying how much she enjoyed her visit. Whether it was the fairies or not, Ellen never received another silent phone call, and her fairy dell flourished. The same could be said of Ellen, who began to appreciate the little things - a lovely sunset or a fluffy cloud, the flowers that grew despite the city traffic, or the song of a blackbird in the park - any little touch of magic.

198

Finbar the Fish

*L*ast night my water was disturbed by that subtle shimmering that I find so unsettling. I swam around the tank for a while, but I could not shake off that heavy feeling that always accompanies these vibrations. Eventually they stopped, but I am convinced that all is not well, and that the problem lies with Sorcha. I have been with her for so long now that I can gauge her mood very accurately when she comes close to the tank and especially if she touches the sides or dips a finger in the water. It is surprising how much information the water carries to me, even through the sides of the tank. When she sprinkles food onto the water every morning and evening I can usually tell what mood she is in, and lately I have been worried about her.

I remember when I first came to live with Sorcha I had a smaller home, shaped like a globe. Sorcha would often put both her hands around my home and lift it up. Somehow the shape seemed to amplify the vibrations emanating from her hands and I soon learnt to interpret them. In those days she seemed happy. The vibrations were stimulating. I have always believed that those energising vibrations from Sorcha helped me to recover from my ordeals. I don't like to recall the time before I lived with Sorcha, it was so unpleasant. I was confined to a tiny piece of water in which I could barely turn round, and was constantly moved and buffeted about. It is no wonder I was weak and dispirited when I got to Sorcha's, but her vibrant energy reached me through the globe and helped me to recover.

Now it seems that Sorcha needs my help. I have tried to send positive energy to her by shaking my fins in the appropriate manner when she feeds me, but it does not seem to have any effect. It may be that her sadness has affected me and that I am unable to produce the correct vibrations, or perhaps she is unable to receive them. It is hard for me to judge, for even though I have learned a great deal about her world, there is much that I do not understand. It was a long time before I understood that when she leant over my water and disturbed the surface with little puffs of air she was trying to communicate with me,

199

and even longer before I could interpret the words that cause the puffs of air. I discovered that she called me Finbar, or sometimes Finbar the Fish. In the mornings and evenings, when she fed me, Sorcha would usually say 'Hello Finbar, how are you?' Because this was repeated so often, I became familiar with its meaning and gradually discerned other words. One word which occurred quite often was 'Amanda'. Its meaning was a puzzle to me until one afternoon Sorcha came to my tank with another girl and said 'Hello Finbar, this is Amanda'. Sorcha picked up the tub of food and tipped some into the Amanda's hand. She sprinkled the food on my water and the Amanda put the food in her hand on the water too. I rose to the surface to suck in some of the food, and was surprised that the Amanda put some fingers into the water and agitated it violently. Sorcha would never do such a thing, and it was quite a shock to me. I did not like the Amanda, and later tried to analyse the information about her that must have been present in the water amid all that disturbance. There was something unpleasant there, apart from the physical agitation of the water - a desire to dominate, control.

Sorcha was happy at that time and her talk of Amanda was enthusiastic. Gradually this changed. The Amanda was not mentioned so often. I remember before I lived with Sorcha, during that awful period when I was confined to an inadequate scrap of water, my tiny water-patch was placed next to another which also contained a fellow fish. Our portions of water were self-contained, and we could not reach one another, even though we were so close. All we could do was gaze at one another and wave a fin now and then. I remember how magnificent my neighbour seemed to me. I admired the way he shook his tail and the heroic look in his eye. He did not seem to be cowed by our circumstances, and his spirit seemed to defiantly transcend our pitiable confinement. I thought him a true hero, a fish who could inspire others, who I would try to emulate. Even though we could not communicate, just to look at him gave me strength and resolve. After such a long time, I still remember my feeling of disappointment when he left me, disappearing without a backward glance, abandoning me to my cruel fate. I felt more lonely, more dispirited than ever. I think that something like this happened to Sorcha. Maybe she saw Amanda in a heroic light, but was abandoned just as I was. Maybe she suffered hardships that I cannot know during the time she is away from me, between feeding me in the morning and the evening. Certainly I could feel her depression.

Yet I feel there is still hope. This morning when she fed me I paid particular attention to her, and could sense a fierce determination, even though it was overlaid with sorrow and apprehension. I feel that today she will take some action to resolve her dilemma. I am quite beside myself as I await her return, and fervently hope that she is successful in her bid to release herself from her sorrows.

I am filled with dread and foreboding. When Sorcha returned it was clear that her plan had not been successful. Indeed it seems that her predicament is worse than ever. When she entered the room she did not come to speak with me, but flung herself down in the place where she sleeps at night. Once again I felt that dreadful shimmering of the water that I have felt for so many nights recently. Now I could also see the shaking of Sorcha's body, confirming my suspicion that Sorcha's unhappiness was the source of the unpleasant vibrations. Eventually she rose and came to feed me. 'Oh Finbar,' she said after she had sprinkled food on the water, 'you wouldn't like me if you knew what I have done. What a fool I've been. I thought they would like me. I did what they wanted, but they pretended to be shocked and horrified. Worse still, Sister Maria found out and is bound to tell my parents. I can't bear the shame, Finbar, we'll have to run away.'

While I was trying to assimilate this, Sorcha went away, returning in a few minutes with a jar of water. She took up the net in which she scoops me up when she refreshes the water in my tank, and dipped it into my water. Apprehensively, I swam into it and allowed her to lift me out. She put me into the jar of water, which was very small and reminded me of that hateful scrap of water I had once been confined in. I made a great effort not to become alarmed. For Sorcha's sake I must stay calm. I knew something strange was happening. This was not the usual procedure when Sorcha refreshed my water, and anyway it did not need doing. Sorcha put on a coat and gently picking up the jar with me in it said 'Come on Finbar, its just you and me now.'

She carried me out of the room where I had lived for so long, and down a jolting slope. I needed all my resolve to remain calm, what with the movement of the jar, which agitated the water, and the unusual sights and smells which constantly unfolded before me. It was difficult for me to make much sense of what they might be. My overwhelming impression was of movement, with constant small shakes of the jar I was in. It was not a pleasant experience, but for Sorcha's sake I tried to bear it stoically.

At last the jolting movements stopped, and I was able to examine my surroundings carefully and try to make sense of them. Sorcha was very close and as I swam around my jar I could see that she was on one side and underneath the jar. She did not speak or move, remaining very still. On the side of the jar away from her body there was a light-coloured band that seemed to be in constant movement. It appeared to move unceasingly from left to right as I watched it, and from the right came a low roaring sound. I had never seen anything like it before, but somehow realised that this moving band was water, the element with which I was so familiar. Yet this water was not confined to a tank — it flowed continually. I wondered where the water went, and felt the urge to follow it. I had never known water that was free of confinement, and imagined that it was hurrying to some magnificent place where waters long to be. As a water creature I yearned to go to this heaven of water, too.

Suddenly, I became aware that Sorcha was also excited. I could feel the tension in her body. Perhaps she too relished the prospect of journeying to that heavenly water-place. It seems that I may have been right, for she leant over my jar and said, 'You're my only friend, Finbar, so I'm going to stick with you. Maybe you can help turn me into a mermaid.'

I did not understand what she meant, but almost immediately she got up and moved towards the water, carrying the jar with her. As we approached the water my excitement grew. How I longed to be in that masterly flow of water! And suddenly I was! Sorcha plunged into the water taking me with her, still in my jar. As the water mingled with that in the jar new sensations assailed me. First the coldness, then strange tastes, and the pull that dragged me with it. What a sensation! As though the water heaven was drawing me towards it. I was happy to go, but remembered Sorcha and tried to turn to see where she was. This was more difficult than I expected. I was used to the still water of a tank and found it difficult to control my movements in this water that pulled me along. Nevertheless I felt that the pull I felt would also carry Sorcha in the same direction. Happy at this thought, I allowed myself to go with the flow, luxuriating in the feeling of freedom. I found that as I no longer fought against the pull I could turn enough to see Sorcha. She seemed totally at ease, relaxed, as she let the water carry her to her destiny, her long black hair dancing about her in the flow. The speed of the flow seemed to increase, and Sorcha and I, after a moment's hesitation, passed over an edge and cascaded down with the water that poured over. Over we went, together, towards an exciting new adventure.

Gilbert Morrey
Inishfree Writers

Bewitched

*J*t was a relief to reach the shade of the palm tree. 'Not that there's much shelter under a palm tree,' muttered Ruby. 'And anyway these people planted the tree too close to their house. The poor thing has no room to spread.'

She gazed upwards into the fronds and that's when she discovered the witch's broom, untidily growing, squatting like a settlement of bird's nestings.

'Cluttered-looking affair, you are,' she told it.

A large marmalade cat poked its head over the edge of the clutter and said:

'I could say the same about you. In fact, you're quite dishevelled. I suppose you always talk to yourself when you're standing under a palm tree?'

Ruby thought for a minute or two. A talking cat! There's no such thing, not unless —

'You must be a witch!'

The cat yawned, but no reply was forthcoming.

'I don't know what else you could be, but if you are a witch, you ought to be black.'

'Who says?'

'I do.'

'Well, Ruby, it's a matter of personal opinion.'

'It's none of your business, who I am.'

'Oh, yes, it is. I'm quite partial to parking myself in this tree. I don't like to be disturbed by a Ruby or anything else.

'Grumpy, aren't you?'

'Not particularly — and, by the way, I'm not a witch.'

'You've got to be, or we couldn't be having a conversation.'

'I'm a warlock, and my name is Desmond. Please refer to me as Desmond in future.'

'I hope I don't have to refer to you at all. I only stepped under this tree to hide from someone who's been bothering me.'

'I suppose that's the spotted Richard who lives in the next street!'

Ruby gasped, and stared for a few moments. 'How do you know things ... like my name being Ruby and that my boyfriend's name is Richard?'

The cat flipped a paw and batted its nose. 'You'd be surprised how much I know. I know lots of things. For instance I know you look lovely when you're sleeping ... all that wavy, black hair, spread out and flowing over the pale pillows.'

Ruby stared again. She could not make this out at all. Was it a spoof of some sort?

'You'd need to have been in my bedroom to see me when I'm asleep.'

'That's an easy one. It's no trouble at all for me to run up the fronts of houses and slip inside open bedroom windows.'

'Oh! Go away, and leave me to hide in peace. I'm not listening to you any more.'

'Suits me fine. You're the one who disturbed my doze.'

Desmond curled himself up in a ball and closed his eyes. Ruby remained where she was, every now and again looking to the right, watching for Richard to come seeking her. Richard was an old fart really, always fussing, always telling her what to do. She had no desire to marry him and settle down as he always asked. In fact she did not want to marry anybody.

A free spirit was what she wanted to be, to roam here and there and amuse herself whichever way pleased her at any particular moment in time. Above all else, she coveted a go at controlling the wind, switching it around and making it blow in the opposite direction. She had a yearning to study the reactions of ordinary people as they were confronted by such a phenomenon. When she pulled faces as a child, she remembered her mother warning: 'If the wind changes, your face'll stay like that.' Now she wanted to make it happen.

Excitement, out of the ordinary events - she craved them all. It was this longing for excitement that caused the row with Richard. They had been walking along Cherryvalley Avenue when Ruby noticed the pony grazing in someone's garden.

'Come on, Richard. Let's mount and ride him off into the distance. I'll sit to the front and you sit to the back.'

'I'll do no such thing,' he retorted narkily. 'Likely the horse belongs to the people who live in that house. What do you think they'll do if you just go in and get up on its back?'

'Well then, if we can't go off on its back, let's tie its mane in knots... that'll give its owners something to think about.'

'Certainly not. Control yourself, woman.'

Ruby pouted. 'I might have known you'd never agree. Well! I'm off, and don't you dare follow me.' And she had dashed away as fast as she could.

Fifteen more minutes passed and it occurred to Ruby that he had not followed her. 'Good. I think I'll go home now.' But just before she started to make tracks, a voice suddenly shattered the quietness.

'Des-mond. Des-mond.' The voice began the *Des* part down in base, and travelled up the scale until it finished the last *dih* somewhere close to treble C.

Ruby waited to see how Desmond would respond. Within minutes he stretched and purred. 'Well, I suppose I'd better go. She might have a saucer of milk waiting for me and, I must confess, I'm quite incredibly thirsty.'

'Who is she?'

'Oh, she's the woman of the house. She thinks she owns me. Little does she know I could dine on the finest caviare any time I so desired.'

'Why don't you, then?'

'I will, when it suits me. I'll take you with me, if you like.'

'I don't like.'

'Suit yourself then. But don't forget... leave your bedroom window open. I'll be seeing you.'

After Desmond had entered the house through what seemed to be his favourite way of getting into a place — an open bedroom window — Ruby stayed on for a while. She suddenly felt at a bit of a loss, almost like the old song her grandpa sometimes sang, *I took my harp to a party and nobody asked me to play.*

Eventually, she picked up the tail of her long black skirt and legged it along the road to her own home. She went straight up to her bedroom and leaned out of the window, staring at the palm tree where she had lately sheltered. But there was no sign of either Desmond or Richard.

She was just about to have a bath and go to bed when her mother called:

'You're awanted down here, our Ruby. Your cousin's come

205

round. She's got a wart that's ripe for the charming.'

Ruby wrinkled up her nose. What a reputation to acquire, the charming away of warts. She could not remember the first one she had dealt with but obviously she must have been successful for people had been bringing their warts ever since.

Downstairs she examined the ugly little growth on her cousin's finger, then went to the drawer and fetched a piece of string. She tied a knot in it and touched the wart lightly with the knot before handing the string to her cousin.

'You take this piece of string and throw it over your left shoulder into the pond at midnight. As the string rots, so shall your wart dwindle.'

Brushing aside a bundle of *thank-yous*, Ruby told her mother:

'I'm going to bed, and I don't want to be disturbed again, especially not for any more old warts or the like. I'm tired.'

Ruby fell asleep quickly, and — it seemed in no time at all — was dreaming that a handsome young man stood beside her. He had long auburn hair, and the most startling of green eyes. He laughed:

'Ha, Ruby. You don't know whether I'm here, or if it's all a dream. Come with me, take my hand, and we'll fly over the fields and far away. Far, far away. Far away to my castle, and we'll have fun. You like fun, don't you?'

'No, don't try to answer me. Everywhere will be black and misty, just the conditions you're happiest with, and the castle, oh, stand back and take a good look at my castle. It has zodiac signs all around the walls. And the courtyard? Why the courtyard's laid out in the design of a chess board. You and me, Ruby, we could crawl about playing chequers and, afterwards, we'll relax, sipping our liqueurs. One that's chocolate and coffee-based is my favourite, with just a little smidgeon of cream on top. We'll stretch out in front of a roaring fire and then... but I'll leave *then* to your imagination.'

Ruby stirred and stretched out her hand towards the lovely young man, but he just suddenly disappeared.

'Was I dreaming? Or was he real? And if he was real, it's all very peculiar.'

Wide awake now, she reflected on the strange things that always appeared to be happening to her. The first one she actively remembered was when she was four years old. Her mother had been pushing her young brother in a pram. Ruby, as usual, dallied behind, creating little stories. A hole in the dug-up road attracted her and she stood beside it peering down. It was a deep, deep hole. To her amazement Zulu warriors, wearing scant, bright skirts, were performing a war dance down there. She could see their black bodies gleaming with sweat. She had stared and stared, and then one looked up and saw her, and made a grab as if to pull her in along with them. Ruby had taken off, running after her mother, clutching at the pram and sobbing out her tale.

'Oh, our Ruby, you're a strange girl all right ... a strange girl ... like nobody else I've ever encountered. But maybe a wee bit like your granny. Now she was another strange girl.'

Ruby lay staring at the ceiling. Her heart thudded at the remembrance of a young man with green eyes and long auburn hair. Would she ever see him again? She hoped so.

As for Richard, now she scarcely allowed him even the smallest window in her deliberations. 'I hope he just goes off to the moon. I really can't be bothering with him again.'

Next day, she returned to the palm tree.

'Are you there, Desmond?'

'Of course, I'm here. This is my favourite place, except for when I'm far away in a place of dark mists in a wonderful old castle that I own.'

'So, you were in my bedroom last night?'

'What makes you think so?'

'Oh, I had a visit from someone, who seemed to offer me all that I wanted.'

'I hope you're going to accept his offer.'

'I'm thinking about it. I'm just going to take my shoes off, and lie down under this palm tree, and ponder for a while.'

Ruby slipped off her shoes, wriggled her toes, all eleven of them, six of them on her left foot, and concentrated. There was mother to consider. But somehow she did not think there'd be too much heartbreak in that quarter. Ruby knew her mother often regarded her as a bit of a nuisance with odd, peculiar ways that nobody else's daughter seemed to possess. In fact, she often felt herself to be quite an embarrassment.

'Just like your grandmother,' was a remark sometimes directed Ruby's way. Unfortunately, it always sounded like Grandmother had not met with much approval either.

And there were all the warty cousins too. 'Honestly, I never knew any one family to be so afflicted by warts. Och! They'll soon find somebody else who's custodian of a charm. You can find such a person in all kinds of places.'

She wriggled her toes again. She had made up her mind.

'Here's to metamorphosis!' she shouted, just before the flash which signalled her transformation into a sleek, black cat.

Rhoda Watson
Newtownabbey Writers' Group

rainbows dolphins and crabs

why go looking

for it

when you have

already found it

hang a few prisms

in the window

to charm the sunlight

into giving up

its rainbows

two dolphin swim

by so quickly

that nobody

sees them

but me

everywhere i walk

on the sandy beach

seaweed and crabs

zen garden

i tried one rock

looked great

tried two rocks

then three

looked terrible

tried one rock again

looked just right

the essence of simplicity

a perfect place

a perfect place

to meditate

watching the sea

a black seal

popping up and down

his nose high

up in the air

i sit legs crossed

quietly playing my clarinet

the high notes

shimmering

over a perfect sea

bits and pieces

a large

white fluffy cloud

leaf-shaped

when i look back

it's gone

just bits and pieces

or should i say crumbs!

barry edgar pilcher
inishfree writers

Struttin' his Stuff

Between times when he was not engaged in shouting gospel messages and startling the life out of unsuspecting passers-by, Joshua McSorley spent his days looking for sin.

He prowled about the city of Belfast — and no word other than prowled suited his particular manner of going about — as he peered here and there, giving people filthy looks. Folk were often alarmed and put at odds with themselves when they accidentally caught Joshua's eye and encountered his baleful expression.

Max Glover caught one of the looks one morning on his way into the office, and it put him off his stroke for the rest of the day.

At coffee time he told his PA: 'That creature has a screwed-up, whingey look on his dial that's absolutely ferocious.'

'Oh I know,' said she, 'I always go out of my road to avoid him, for he terrifies me the way he suddenly roars through that loudhailer, "You're all going to hell." Maybe I am, but if I am, I'd rather not know about it. I wonder what makes men of his age go in for such behaviour. You'd think he'd want to sit by a fire and watch television, instead of coming out in the cold and the wet. But I ought not to be surprised, this city's bothered by a great abundance of such people.'

Sometimes Joshua himself wondered why he paid for Gospel tracts out of his own pocket and trailed out every day to shout at citizens, all of whom appeared hell-bent on ignoring him and getting on with life in their own sinful ways.

Deep down, really, he knew the answer. It was fun. He was getting back at everybody who had ever annoyed him in his previous seventy years: all those bosses who'd treated him like a go-for. He was having the fun now that he'd missed out on in earlier times.

Before he left his back-street home in the mornings, he delighted in hunting through the Bible, trying to find a sentence he had not come across previously. The more fear-provoking connotations it contained, the better. For Joshua, such words could never be frightening enough.

'There's sin everywhere. The whole world has turned into Sodom and Gommarah,' he muttered to his cat.

The cat ignored him. Its only interest in life was a well-filled bowl, and a warm, comfortable cushion, and for that it put up with a lot of ranting and raving. Joshua liked to practise testimonies in the living room, going on until the people next door, driven to distraction, banged on the wall with a mallet.

'I've got to get it right tomorrow... people are fast going to the devil. They need shocking out of their contentment,' he told the cat.

The next day was Saturday and he liked Saturdays best of all. On Saturdays, buskers, Hare Krishna devotees, cigarette lighter vendors and all kinds of people vied for space around Cornmarket. On a Saturday Joshua always polished his shoes carefully, gave his tabard-like over-jacket a damp wipe and re-outlined the text printed in white letters. He even brushed his paddy hat and dusted his loud-hailer. Right now he looked in the mirror and the image seemed to shimmer so that he was not looking at the usual screwed-up face but a younger version of himself.

He sighed, memory nudging backwards to Freda and their last meeting.

'It's goodbye Josh,' she'd said. 'I can't take all your constant harping on about religion. I like wearing make-up and jewellery and I'll be keeping my skirt as short as I want to. I can't see what any of this has to do with religion.'

He sighed again. Years later he'd caught a glance of her and three small children in the crowd and he'd roared *you're all going to hell*, with more venom than usual. But she had not turned her glance in his direction.

The bus he boarded was filled with young men, obviously on the way to a football match, and young women with hair dyed every colour in the rainbow.

'They'll be sorry one day when the flames of hell're licking round their heels,' he told himself.

Just before leaving the bus he paused on the platform, and shouted: 'You'll be laughing with the other sides of your faces when the day of judgement comes.'

'Aye, all right, right on, Daddy-o,' came from the only guy who paid the slightest attention.

It took Joshua ten minutes to reach the main square but when he reached his favourite spot he was incensed to see a Hare Krishna-ite standing on it. He pushed right up to the man and grabbed a handful of his robe.

214

'You'll have to move somewhere else. This is my place.'

The man looked him up and down gently. 'Who says?' he eventually enquired.

'I do.'

Joshua's internal fuse burned out with a whoosh.

'You take yourself off, you big baldy git - standing there, wearing a dress, like some ould Jinny.'

The punch came out of nowhere.

Joshua looked up from the wet ground where he lay and appealed to the onlookers.

'Look at him, the big hairless harry. All he's good for is hitting old men.'

But he shut up quickly as the man pushed a clenched fist under his nose and mouthed a few further threats.

Police were on the scene quickly and Joshua was booked for disturbing the peace.

He's not allowed to preach in public any more, but he still goes down the town every day, glaring here and glaring there, looking for sin, and finding it everywhere that he looks.

John Wesley, the cat, came off worst for now it has to listen all day to the roaring of testimonies. The animal always feels a great sense of relief when it hears the sound of a mallet striking the wall next door.

Rhoda Watson
Newtownabbey Writers' Group

Spring Model

From fat pubescent bud, we watched you grow.
To yellow-headed beauty only Nature could bestow.

Golden-topped and slender, sashaying in the breeze
With classic green accessories you know just how to please.

Tall and graceful daffodil, adornment for short season
Why do you last so short a time? — *My beauty is the reason.*

Community Alert

*T*he unthinkable happened a month ago. My elderly neighbour's house was broken into and ransacked, while she was held captive. Although it is the sort of incident one hears about increasingly, it is not the sort of incident one expects in this peaceful rural area of Donegal, in broad daylight while people are still going about their usual daily business.

My friend, Mary, lived in a remote country place along a single-track lane. Her house is in full view of two neighbouring houses, where the inhabitants could be described as 'very interested', or even 'nosey', neighbours. (Remoteness and lack of overt action tends to have this effect on people.) It is the sort of place where the hall door is never locked until dark, and where the postman comes right into the house with the letters.

Mary, my friend, was in her eightieth year — alert, independent and capable. The day of the incident was a normal day for her. She had been busy in the garden and had just come indoors to make herself a cup of tea. She thought she heard the postman and started towards the door — only to be confronted by a large hooded figure.

She didn't even have time to think. She was bundled into the bathroom with a hand clapped over her mouth. Her hands were tied behind her back and a nylon scarf secured tightly over her eyes. Not a word was spoken. All she could hear was the sound of frantic activity and the beating of her own heart.

Then she heard the key being turned in the bathroom door. At least, she was alive! She could tell that there were people moving about the house by the swish of their quick movements. She thought she heard furniture being moved and apart from some rustling and scratching sounds and the banging of the front door, there was nothing …

She was thankful to God that she was not hurt. She longed to go to the toilet but she could not for her hands were securely tied. She felt her way to the toilet seat and sat down on the lid. All she could do was wait until somebody came.

Sure enough when night came, I, being one of the nosey neighbours, noticed that Mary's lights were not on. When she did not answer the telephone, I went to investigate and knew at a glance that something was wrong. Finding Mary was my first priority and then I phoned the police who were on the scene quickly.

Mary was shaken but calm, relieved to be rescued and unharmed. Of course, anything which could be redeemed for money, had gone. Her handbag and small strongbox containing her legal and domestic documents were her most serious loss.

She reckoned that the intruders had been in the house about five minutes. 'It could have been so much worse,' we consoled her. Although her house had been ransacked and property stolen, she had not been abused, either physically or mentally.

But how true was that? Over the past month, I watched her decline. She changed from being cheerful and outgoing to being watchful and over-anxious. All her spontaneity and *joie de vivre* had gone. The worry of replacing documents and reorganising her lifestyle, with the emphasis on security, weighed heavily on her. Her eyes had a haunted look. She, who had been so tidy and well organised, looked sleepless and dishevelled.

She had chosen not to move from her house. She had chosen not to be professionally counselled. Always a private and independent person, she wanted to reconstruct her own life. She didn't want to talk about the horror of the incident, although she would talk about the practical difficulties of replacing stolen items.

Informal arrangements were made for neighbours to call with her daily, and of course there was always the telephone. It was no comfort to her that the intruders had 'done' two houses ten miles away, the same late afternoon, using the same tactics and again targeting old people, living alone. Now a Community Alert System has been instituted in the area.

Again, last night, at lighting-up time there was no light in Mary's window. I tried to telephone her. There was no reply. I went to her house. This time the door was locked.

Through the window, I could see her slumped in a chair by the fireside.

In the meantime, three adults (two men and a woman) have been charged with the break-ins which took place on that day. I hope they will also be charged with manslaughter.

Shirley Ohlmeyer
Inishfree Writers

Sarah's Gate

An excerpt

"Clart!" retorted Sarah Cruickshank, as she fixed the net on her living room window. She had been nebbing out the window of her flat as usual and had not been disappointed in what she saw.

"Dirty big gop, good for nothin' other than scrubbin' out toilets. That one should be neutered! Wud ye luk at the pockle's of that big glipe, what th' hell men see in 'er is a mystery. To hell an' she falls on her arse for that's where her brains are."

She let the curtain fall back into place, and pottered towards her chair and plopped herself down, her spindly legs went up and down like pistons as she positioned her skinny feet into her extra wide carpet slippers. Her bunion had been throbbing for weeks and it was making her more bad tempered than usual, although it didn't take much to put our Sarah into a bad mood.

"Don't go casting aspersions about what you don't understand, mother. You know nothing about the woman apart from what you conjure up in that over fertile brain of yours."

Elsie Friars glared at Sarah in disgust and adjusted her glasses so they sat snugly on the bridge of her nose. She held the *Sun* newspaper slightly to the left of herself so as the weak winter sun that shone through her mother's netted window in the small living room would be an aid to her ailing eyesight.

"I know plenty, our Elsie. I wasn't born yesterday, ye know. Men would go with anythin' that wore a skirt. Put a beg over her head an' after half a bottle of whiskey no man would say no. Although, God knows, they would have to be desperate. The woman doesn't even know what soap or deodorant's for, never mind how to use it. Disinfectant and bleach must never be on her shoppin' list. Her house must be piggin' inta the bargain."

"Her house is not dirty. Rab cleans it as well as Peggy. Rab was in the army you know, anyone who's been in the army is very meticulous about their hygiene," retorted Elsie. She removed her glasses and

219

squinted at her mother, huffing like a bull in a rage at the same time. Without her glasses Elsie was almost blind, and at times she looked on it as a blessing. If she took her glasses off, her mother was nothing other than a blur, which suited her down to the ground as the sight of her made her feel ill. Her mother's bitterness showed itself in her screwed-up face, and her wizened body resembled a dried-up corpse at times. Elsie often wondered what held it together apart from sinew and bone.

"Aye, meticulous and shifty," replied Sarah, puckering her lips after she made this much thought out observation. "In for a whiplash claim an' he can turn that neck of his full circle. If ye ask me he's nothin' other than a crook."

"I'm not asking you anything, ma. Rab would run to the ends of the earth for anyone, including you, and you know it. His legs are run off him over the head of that flamin' gate of yours."

"He's the dregs of humanity!" snapped Sarah.

"God forgive ye, ma. He's a human being. He has feelings like everyone else. Everyone apart from yourself, who has feelings for no-one. At least he doesn't go running people down all the time. You have to give a bit of lee-way now an' then ye know. I'm the one who has to pick up the pieces when you blow your top, ma, an' that's becoming a regular occurrence these days."

Elsie turned the page of her newspaper. She replaced her glasses but had lost the thread of what she had been reading. She folded the newspaper and threw it onto the floor with a sigh. Trying to read in Sarah's company was futile.

"You're puttin' me into an early grave, do ye know that?" screeched Sarah.

"An early grave! Good heavens, ma, you're in your eighties. If anyone's goin' to an early grave it will be Rab. He's barely turned fifty an' he has a bad heart an' lungs, and before you say it he never smoked or drank in his life."

"Neither did yer da, an' he died at seventy. An' I am not old, I'm mature!"

"If you're mature, ma, I'm an infant. An' there's a hell of a difference between fifty an' seventy!" rebuked Elsie. "And another thing. My da didn't suffer like Rab. He died in his sleep. He probably didn't know a thing about it."

Sarah reneged. "Well I suppose he's not too bad." She huffed for a few seconds as she thought about Peggy. "But that Peggy one is nothin' other than a trollop!" She then got up from her chair and started dusting with a rag that she kept in her apron pocket, then she began fidgeting with the ornaments, a sure sign that she had lost the argument.

Elsie rested her elbow on her knee to steady her right arm. Her frayed nerves had her shaking to the marrow, as Sarah had done nothing other than bad mouth the world and its wife for the past two hours. She had been up since the crack of dawn attending to Sarah's needs, delivering her newspaper and gathering up her bits and pieces that needed to be washed, for Sarah didn't have a washing machine. A phone call had got her up an hour earlier that day. Sarah had rung at half seven to inform her of the previous night's snowfall and that the end of the world must be coming as the street looked so dead. Would she come over and keep her company? Elsie felt so tired and peeved off she wished the end of the world was nigh so she could have a few hour's extra kip of a morning. Sure the flaming estate looked dead every morning, why was today so different? No, it was only an excuse to get her over early, an extra hour of listening to Sarah's incessant bitching about how every person in the news was either a degenerate, a thief or a scoundrel. According to Sarah every female in show business must have had more nips and tucks and face-lifts than hot dinners.

"I'd have had my own face lifted only it would have dropped again at the price," Sarah informed her daughter, who was now ready for screaming, her nerves were that jangled.

Elsie squinted out of the corner of her eye at Sarah and thought to herself, it would take Harland and Wolff shipyard workers to do the scaffolding, your face is that dropped.

Sarah had taken two Pro-plus earlier on in the morning. They gave her energy and her mouth was now firing on all cylinders. The extra caffeine had the effect of a lubricant on her tongue.

She glared at her daughter who had once again lifted the newspaper in another bid to read.

"As for the nude model on the third page of that newspaper yer lookin' at, don't they realise breasts are fer feedin' youngsters an' not fer the titillation of randy auld gets. Standin' there without a runion on, ye wid think sex had only been invented." Sarah's face puckered up in disgust as she tried to pry the newspaper away from Elsie's hands as if she were a dirty old man caught in the act of some sexual deviancy.

"Catch yourself on, give me back my newspaper," snapped Elsie. "You must have had your moments, for you had more than your allocated share of two-point-four children in your lifetime. I'm sure you felt a flutter when you rode on the pillion of your dearly intended.

Don't tell me you just sat and held hands astride his bike an' picked daisies in the woods at the end of the day."

The look of disgust turned to one of horror at Elsie's insinuations.

"Don't you dare accuse me of gettin' up to shenanigans or of being over-sexed. Anyway, my husband had a job, remember."

"What has a job got to do with it?" asked Elsie in amazement. "Does a job entitle one to more nookie than those who are unemployed?"

Elsie changed position. She plumped up a cushion, and tucking her legs up under herself, laid her head down on the cushion hoping the softness would ease the headache she could feel starting at the back of her neck. Sarah rambled on. She had no sympathy for others in pain, even though she herself moaned about every ailment imaginable, from constipation to the nipping ulcer on her ankle. An ulcer the size of a pinhead. This gave her something in common with the Queen Mother, who supposedly suffers from the same malady. So either she felt an empathy or else she felt entitled to lord it in front of her neighbours, who were fed up with the hoity-toity voice she put on when riled.

"People who are unemployed should not have children!" Sarah hit the arm of her chair with her fist and her eyeballs nearly shot out of her head. "They should abstain from all that auld carry-on, put their energy where it's needed. Years ago they would be trampin' the streets in shoes worn to the uppers with a lunch tucked under their oxters in search of work, instead of cafufflin' about between the sheets."

"God, would you listen to it. Past her three score years and ten and talkin' about sex. And just exactly what would your answer be to the thousands of unemployed in Ireland who felt the urge to engage in a little bit of the other?"

Sarah glared at Elsie in utter horror. "The other" was not in her vocabulary, in fact anything referring to the act of sex was not "nice talk".

"The women should have all taken away after having two young-sters, or else the men should all be castrated!" This was Sarah's way of referring to a hysterectomy. She hirpled over to the window and pulled back the lace curtain. She started tut-tutting and with a beckoning of her index finger called Elsie over to witness the antics that were going on across the road.

Two teenagers were engaged in a romantic embrace in the doorway of a house opposite the flats.

"Now that's what puts bad thoughts into the young, standin' there birdlin' in broad daylight, kissin' and feelin' each others bums. They get it from their parents, ye know. Did you know that child's mother lets that young lad stay th' night? He must sleep with that wee hussy, for the rest of the youngsters take up the other rooms along with all the other degenerates who call with their carry-outs from the off licence. It's only eleven in the mornin'. He must have stayed th' night and now he's goin' home to his own house to lie in his pit for the rest of the day an' scrounge off his parents. Bloody vampires, stay up all night, then sleep all day. Sure ye would know they are vampires: their necks are covered in bites. The next thing ye will see is thon mother of hers wheelin' the pram up the street while that wee tramp lies in bed snatterin' all day. The youngen's aren't content till they have a buggie or some other contraption wi' a chile gurnin' in it. The mothers an' fathers have no shame in today's society. They probably flaunt their animalistic antics in front of their weans instead of keepin' it behind closed doors like me an' my husband did. Ach, an-nee an' an-nee, what's the world comin' to?"

She collapsed into her armchair and wiped her forehead with the corner of her apron. Her speech on the depravity of the teenagers of today had left her exhausted. She asked Elsie to put the kettle on for a cup of tea as her throat felt dry.

For a moment Elsie hoped her talking had tired her out. She might have a wee doze and give her ears a rest.

"Not a bit of wonder your throat's dry. That was near enough as long as President Clinton's and the mayor's speech put together at Christmas, and that was as big a waste of time as you trying to persuade the young to abstain from sex. Your husband was my father in case you've forgotten, so come down from your high horse and let me read this paper in peace. Birdlin'! Where the hell did you get that expression from? You must have a very fruitful imagination, not to mention disgusting. Now who's talkin' sex? And, by the way, it is not animalistic as you so eloquently put it." Elsie said the word in a sarcastic tone which annoyed Sarah even more.

"It is!" Sarah yelled back, her voice taking on a new resonance. She sounded almost hysterical, like a DUP politician held captive at a Sinn Fein conference. "There should have been other ways to have weans."

"What other way can you have children? They don't appear from the blue, you know. The last time that happened there was a bright star in the east while the shepherds watched their flocks by night."

"Don't mock religion, our Elsie." Sarah yapped back. "Anyway, ye could adopt a child if ye were that desperate. God knows there are enough orphans in the world."

Elsie laughed at her mother's logic. "And just where do you think the children come from that are up for adoption? And you're the one that runs down religion, not me. So remember that in future, if you don't mind."

"From under-educated natives that know no better. The heat makes them do 'it' or 'the other', as you might say. I'm sure I don't know where you got that language from, ye girl ye. Marrying below yourself I suppose. An' I don't run down religion. I just don't believe all that much in it. Not when you look at the state of the world."

"Then all the children would be coloured and that would be another fault in your eyes. Sex is not only to have children, you know."

Elsie could have bitten her tongue off for she knew she had risked provoking her mother even further, but decided to go for gold. "It is an expression of one's love for another. And excuse me, I did not marry below myself, my father did that. And don't blame God for the state of the world. Human beings did that." Elsie prepared herself for a rollicking with this last remark but was surprised at her mother's response.

Sarah looked flustered and shifted uneasily in her chair, picking up imaginary bits of fluff with her fingers, and started wringing the corner of her apron, for she knew this last remark to be true.

"Ah give over. Talkin' nonsense ye are, an' at your age. I hope you an' thon husband of yours have givin up all that auld kissin' an' cuddlin'," she said sheepishly.

Elsie sighed to herself, I've done it again, I've hurt her feelings, now my conscience will be up the left all day. As for sex, well, she had long given up nights spent in unabandoned passion but given the right man, one wouldn't know what erotic behaviour and wanton lust might emerge from her dormant female desires.

At the age of eighty-three Sarah had the eyesight of a hawk, the tongue of a lizard, and ears that could have heard a fly fart in mid flight. Elsie was fifty-seven, she needed glasses, but was as quiet as a mouse, in the company of everyone except her mother. She brought out the worst in Elsie. She was not going to come up for breath now she was on a roll and had started on the Royal family.

"Take the Queen, for example. She won't stand no nonsense, she rules thon family of hers with a rod of iron. Charlie boy has to do what he's told, Diana has no say in the matter. I bet those two boys of theirs would have been the last even if they hadn't have split up. I can't see the Queen being held down with a pack of grandchildren."

Elsie giggled at the scene that flashed before her eyes. The thought of the Queen baby-sitting in curlers, carpet-slippers and sweating cobs as she told William and Harry to keep one's royal mucky mitts off one's family heirlooms in case one wanted a right royal hiding round one's shell-like lug-holes was enough to send the most dour of persons into a fit.

"I don't know what's so funny, our Elsie. After all she's human. She has to pee an' pass wind like the rest of us." She wagged her finger at Elsie who was by now taking as much notice as an eskimo inspecting an air-cooling unit, as she had heard the same story a hundred times before.

"Do you know? I pity thon poor woman. She must be astray in the mind. What, with running the country, that's if you could call it a country now - it's more like a zoo full of animals if ye ask me."

She realised Elsie wasn't listening to her and slapped her on the ear to get her attention. "Will you look at me when I'm talkin' till ye, ye have a habit of ignoring me these days. No time for th' old, I suppose?"

Elsie rubbed her ear, pulled the newspaper up to hide her face and mouthed the words, "By Christ I've better things to look at!", then bit down hard on the boiled sweet she had been sucking in an attempt to help drown out the old woman's incessant bantering with the crunch.

"Of course, I don't think she need worry about Edward, he's too busy making tea in that flamin' theatre company he works for. What will his Royal emblem be - a Tetley tea bag? His da should have made him stay in the Marines. A good kick up the arse would have put the life back into him."

She reminded Elsie that she had not put on the kettle as she pondered on this last remark. "As for Andrew an' Fergie, well, her head must be turned with th' antics they get up to. Then again it's sex talkin'. All the Dukes of York were fly men. What do ye think he gets up to with all them sailors when his boat docks? He's a man just like the rest of them - a girl in every port."

Princess Anne was on the point of getting a tongue-lashing when Sarah spotted a trail of dust on the mantelpiece. Once again she eased herself out of her chair and hirpled towards the kitchen for a duster to vent her frustrations with a bit of polishing.

"Ye could clean this auld flat till ye were blue in the face and it would look no better," she remarked with a bitter tone to her voice. She was thinking of better days when she could boast to all and sundry about her life in a bungalow in a posh area.

Christ! Is she never goin' to give up rabbiting? thought Elsie as she lifted her head from the newspaper that she was once more attempting to read. For a brief moment she glanced at Sarah who was now feverishly polishing a brass candle stick. She visualised the brass object thumping the daylights out of her mother. That would shut her up once and for all. Why the hell had she not even thought of replacing her mother's Pro-Plus with Valium, maybe even popped a dozen or so into her tea? At least it would have shut her up for a few hours. She had a gut feeling her mother would live to see her out the door feet first in a wooden overcoat, and shuddered at the thought of not having a few years' respite to herself without the old moan bending her ear night and day. She was quickly brought to her senses at the thought of spending the rest of her life in jail for murder or attempted poisoning and decided it was not a good idea after all. Sarah had no intentions of letting the grim reaper carry her off without a fight. She fed herself on porridge, with acacia honey as a substitute for sugar. She would often remark, "Honey is more healthy for body an' the soul." She followed this with a more than adequate supply of wheat-bran toasted bread liberally plastered with whiskey-flavoured orange marmalade.

"A good breakfast gets th' auld bowels workin' in the mornin'. Once yer cleaned out in the nether regions the rest af the body, plus the mind, works better."

Her observation must have been spot on as she had a brain that worked at the speed of light. The honey had her buzzing like a bee while the whiskey in her marmalade had her drunk with her own importance. Her body, which now had a dowager's hump and was shrunken with age, still had the strength to swipe the odd back-hander round the ear of anyone who got in her way.

Why, you might be tempted to ask, was Elsie wearing her mother's glasses if Sarah's eyesight was keener than that of a hawk? The answer is simple. Sarah had obtained a pair of reading glasses as a visual aid to snobbery in Castle Court shopping centre on a day trip to Belfast. She had been watching Dame Edna on the television one night, and out of nothing other than sheer ignorance she decided that if a pair of spectacles could help wield a little more power over the lower classes they were definitely an asset to one's outward demeanour. In fact she had gone as far as getting a pair similar to Dame Edna's, which only made her look like a gremlin when she wore them on her shrunken head. Thank God she didn't multiply when she splashed water on herself or Elsie would be completely away in the head with miniature Sarahs hopping about all over the place.

"It's all I've got is the television, not like thon auld gather-up up th' stairs who sits in pubs all night an' would drink out of a shitty reg. She needs a good slap up the bake, spendin' all her money on drink an' not a bite in the house. No wonder she looks like a herrin' with stays on, an' the face the colour of clay. As for that wee crathur next door that's knee high to a fairy, how the hell he got into the Parachute Regiment is a mystery."

She put the candlestick back on the mantelpiece with a thump, turned round and started on Elsie all over again. "See thon wee legs of his, they must have got buried up his arse when he hit the groun' wrong. Five feet nothin' in 'is hob-nail boots he is. Do you ever see his tartles hangin' out on th' washin' line? Woollen underpants darned at the bum. Imagine! Darnin' yer drawers in this day an' age, makes me sick to the stomach it does. Dirt and filth dregged up to know no better. Yer father would turn in 'is grave if he knew where I was livin'." Mind you, this would have been no mean trick as he had been cremated ten years earlier, his ashes having been scattered in the wind.

"For God's sake, ma, give over gabblin'. My head's splittin', squintin' at this newspaper without listening to your mouth goin' a mile a minute. Why aren't you watchin' the television anyway? It's not like you to miss a trick on the box."

"There's nothin' on only bloody children's nonsense, either that or sport. Saturday mornin' is a lot of old b..." She was going to say "bollox" but bit her tongue. She didn't want to lower herself to the language of the other people who lived in the flats. Walls have ears. No, she had to keep some semblance of politeness, even if it killed her.

Elsie's finances did not stretch to the luxury of spectacles.

Her husband, Bert, had been on the dole for the better part of a decade after he had accepted voluntary redundancy at the car factory. Sure he could always do the double in times of dire need. He didn't stop to think. Half of the males in the Ballyhornet estate had thrown their heads back and decided life on the dole would be more rewarding than slogging your guts out or dying of monotony at the end of an assembly line of car parts. Wee jobs on the side were hard to come by now. The dull rows of street upon street of terrace houses of the estate were littered with men scratching their arses and smoking fag ends in front of the television. Each wondered what odd job would save his hide and pay for the weekend's drinking spree, plus a wee flutter on the gee-gees, a go at the football pools and a few quid on the lottery to get the adrenalin going.

If they got five numbers up plus the bonus number, a wee win of a quarter of a million would suffice very nicely.

Poor Elsie, life had not been kind to her. Apart from watching the likes of *Coronation Street* and *Eastenders* and whatever other soap operas the television could spew forth her only other activities were traipsing to the local shops for groceries or visiting close friends. A trip to Belfast was a luxury she could ill afford on Bert's dole money, never mind a holiday. She dreamed of a holiday to Tenerife. A visit to Marks & Spencers was a treat. The sight of flowered toilet rolls and lace-trimmed duvet covers conjured up visions of romantic bedrooms and bathrooms fit for a male Chippendale, and not Bert, whose toes turned up whenever sex entered his mind. This danger signal sent Elsie to the confines of her bathroom for shelter until his ardour cooled.

Elsie was tired to the marrow running to her mother's every whim and fancy without having to lie back and think of Ulster. Anyway, her body had lost its nubile appearance, middle-age spread had hit her with a vengeance and her stomach got in the way of negotiating the joys of sex.

Bert had tried to talk her into trying out new positions in order to get round this obstacle, but Elsie was having none of it. Anything other than the missionary position was out of the question. No way was he going to creep up from behind like a dog. So she would slap him on a most sensitive part of his anatomy with the back of her hand at night and tell him on no uncertain terms to bugger off. He had informed her on one occasion that this was the way to find her "G" spot and she had told him to find a quiet spot instead and take himself in hand! He had huffed for a fortnight and fell into a fit of depression for a few months before resigning himself to the fact that he was no longer regarded as a virile partner by his wife.

Having to go through life with a name that conjured up visions of a maiden aunt was penance enough, without the added insult of letting a man haw and paw her now she was in the menopause.

She had suffered enough indignities in her lifetime. As a child she had a lazy eye and had to wear an ugly-eye patch for years. Her hair was neither blonde nor brown, it was mousey, as her mother often described it. On a Friday night Sarah added insult to injury with her "de-nitting" regime.

"Elsie Cruickshank! Get thon mousy napper of yours over this newspaper till ye get de-loused, and none aff yer moanin' or I'll flay ye till ye know nobody."

Elsie would obey without argument rather than risk the buckle-end of the belt. Sarah loved Friday nights. Being a bit of a battle-axe she could take her bad temper out on a good weekend, when head lice were rampant for some unknown reason. She did this to all six of her children. But Elsie suffered the most because she lacked the golden tresses that adorned her brother's and sister's heads much to her mother's chagrin. Sarah would scrape the fine tooth comb over Elsie's scalp until her head stung as if a horde of wasps had embedded their poisonous barbs in every square inch.

She would then fling Elsie to bed after a bowl of porridge, and mutter, "I can't see the flamin' lice in yer damned hair. The bloody things are as dirty lookin' as the hair they're stickin' to."

So Elsie had to endure the de-lousing ritual until no further lice fell onto the newspaper to be squashed between her mother's thumbnails, accompanied by the cry, "Die, ye buggers, do ye hear me... Die!" She had a habit of talking to anything that moved, even head lice. She also had a field day with blue bottles and flies. The sight of Sarah running round the house with a rolled-up newspaper swatting, swearing and sweating in the confines of her whale-boned corsets in an effort to rid her home of these pests was a novelty not to be missed, except by her husband and children, who felt ashamed when visitors were around. They used to stare at their mother as if she were mental, then look at the family with pity written on their faces. Sticky, brown, fly paper catchers hung from the ceilings of the house like party streamers. They were covered with dead or dying flies and Elsie's father, who was over six foot tall, was forever walking into them face first. This only added to the mayhem in the Cruickshank household of a Friday night as he tried to prise them off his face and out of his hair. While Sarah swore at the nits he swore at Sarah.

"For Christ sake, woman, will you remove these bolloxing flies' graveyards, for it's like walking through the second attack of the Black Plague."

In order to escape into a world of make-believe Elsie spent the better part of her childhood feeding birds and stray dogs, especially mangy ones infested with fleas. As she herself had felt unloved in her early life and knew what it felt like to be deloused, she felt an empathy with them. She took pity on all of God's creatures of the non-human variety and became the patron saint to all the local animals in need of care. Her favourite was a one-eyed cat called Pirate, Pirate being the obvious choice of name for a moggy with this disability.

It did not end with animals. When she was six years old she gave her last Kali sucker to an under-privileged child, as she felt unworthy of having such luxuries, forgetting that she herself was also under privileged, and more than slightly unloved. She grew up feeling guilty at having anything new and accepted other people's cast offs as punishment.

Her gentleness gave her a serenity that showed on her face, and she became a very pretty girl. She had a good facial bone structure, high cheek-bones and heart-shaped face and, before mother nature had robbed her of her twenty-one inch waist with child bearing in later life, she had a figure to die for. Most of the local males had an eye for Elsie at one time or other, but her mother had left her with a legacy of feeling inferior and she spurned their advances, thinking that they were only poking fun at her expense when they wolf whistled in her direction.

But fate always wins in the end. At the age of twenty she met Albert Friars, her ticket to freedom. She felt safe with Bert, at least no one would rob her of his affection. He had a kindly disposition and he showered her with a love she had been denied as a child. A year later they married. No church bells rang out loud, no long black limousines for the bride and groom and family. Just a quiet affair. Elsie and Bert plus two witnesses in a small country church. The only other person present was the Minister, who married them with a look of bewilderment at the lack of guests, not to mention parents. Elsie felt she deserved nothing better, and got on with making the best of her big day. They had a nice dinner in a restaurant, then went back to Bert's parent's house to spend their honeymoon in the back bedroom. Getting married was not going to make her parents love her all of a sudden, so why go to the bother of make believe for the benefit of two people who wouldn't care less if she eloped in the middle of the night with a seven-foot-tall gorilla, as long as it didn't cost them anything.

Thirty-one years and four children plus six grandchildren later, she was reduced to the level of wearing borrowed spectacles, occupying a working kitchen with two odd taps on the sink, and not even enough room to swing a mouse round, never mind the proverbial cat. Ironically she now danced to the tune of her mother's every demand, whilst pondering on the meaning of life, how humans were created and where they went in the hereafter. When some religious boffin came up with another theory, Elsie would muse on their newly-found beliefs with enthusiasm for weeks. She changed religion every other month in her search for the perfect answer to the mystery of life. At one stage she had gone into hospital for an operation as Methodist and came out a Jehovah's Witness a week later. The twenty-odd years of the Troubles had left her with a belief in the existence of spacemen. According to her, they had put us on earth to watch us destroy each other as an experiment. Four-foot-tall grey men were really our rulers. Now that peace had once more been shattered in Ulster, she was convinced a craft from outer space was going to make a landing in the not too distant future and redeem us from this awful planet and take us back to their fold.

When Sarah's husband passed on to better pastures, she sold her precious bungalow and moved to Ballyhornet to be near Elsie. The other two, Helen and Isobel, had managed to escape this misfortune by buying houses in areas that did not cater for pensioners, while her three sons had gone one better and emigrated: clever thinking, although unfair on Elsie, who couldn't say no to a flea-ridden tramp in need of succour, never mind the person who had given her life, albeit a hard one.

The sun disappeared behind a snow cloud, plunging the tiny living room into premature darkness. Elsie removed the spectacles and replaced them with extra care in their blue velvet-covered case for fear they would get scraped, thus giving her mother ammunition for another argument. She sat up straight on the settee and rubbed her tired eyes.

"I'm away over home to make Bert his lunch, ma. Do you need anything from the shops this afternoon?"

Elsie sighed after voicing this last remark as the thought of walking over to the shops on a cold, snowy February afternoon did not cheer her at all. She usually went in the morning but today she felt tired and tetchy and had left it until later in the hope that her energy would take a turn for the better.

"It killed him, ye know." Sarah was staring at a photograph of a young man standing beside an aspidistra plant. The photograph was brown with age and looked out of place beside Sarah's collection of brightly-framed colour snaps of her many grandchildren. Apart from the odd bunch of artificial flowers, her small living room resembled a shrine to a family blessed with fertility. Children's faces adorned every nook and cranny. No Royal Doulton or Ainsley china, just a motley array of seaside ornaments and cheap photographic frames.

It depressed Elsie, who always held the idea that the old should have something to show for their lives, even if it was only the luxury of a nice china tea-set or the odd bit of cut glass. She stifled the urge to scream with frustration for she knew this old ploy of Sarahs. The old photograph trick was only another way of getting her to stay a little longer. Her self-inflicted loneliness, born out of bad temper and jealousy of her neighbours, made her appear pitiful when viewed in the context of her frail exterior. Elsie was gullible when off guard, but today she was not only tired and tetchy. Bert had told her earlier on of his decision to get all his teeth pulled, as they were giving him jip. Christ Almighty! Elsie didn't feel all that romantic towards her husband at the best of times, but this was the last straw. So Elsie was not in the mood to play riddles of what killed who, and why.

"What killed him? For God's sake ma, I didn't even know the man." She hunched forwards and, holding her head in her hands, shook it from side to side and felt like yelling until Sarah came up with the gem.

"Seein' thon man gettin' killed by a bull. Threw him up in the air it did like an auld rag doll, it's bloody horns rammed him straight in the bum, and wiggled him about till the lights were shook out af him. Then it flung him six foot in the air," Sarah indicated his fate by shoving her right thumb in the air.

Elsie's eyes lit up for she enjoyed a good gory story. She sat back in the settee in anticipation of a good old tale of blood and guts and maybe the added titbit of the ghost of the deceased making an appearance, proving that life after death did indeed exist.

"Aye, he couldn't eat nor sleep fer months, his heart gave in as he peddled past the scene on his bike. Willy John Fitzpatrick, a cousin of yer da's he was, one minute full of health and vigour, the next, dead as a doornail wi' fright."

"You mean to say the shock killed him? I never thought you could die of shock. Sure his parents must have been devastated."

"Nat at all, they were long dead."

Elsie's eyes lit up even further. "Are you telling me he was an orphan? He looks very young in the photo." The idea of having an orphan in the family at one time had brightened her day, a little tit-bit such as that would be cause for an afternoon's conversation.

"An orphan! Good God woman, his parents died when he was in his seventies."

"His seventies! In the name of all that's holy, what age was he when he died?"

"A hundred an' one." Sarah answered with a wistful look as if he had been a mere slip of a lad.

"A hundred and one! It was about time he kicked the bucket. In the name of heaven, the man died of old age. Ma, if you make bones as old as his you'll be doin' all right."

"There was a few years left in th' auld boy mind ye, he was still ridin' his bike to work."

"Ridin' his bike! A hundred and one still ridin' his bike. Still workin! Lay off it, ma, me head's splittin'. I'm in no mood for fairy tales."

Valerie Maher
Newtownabbey Writers' Group

232

arranmore

arranmore

looks spectacular

from outside kincasslagh

all of the cottages

to one side

of the island

sheltered away

from the northerly winds

the mighty cliffs stand tall

against the atlantic rollers

the crest of large waves

tipped with white foam

a hokusai wood block print

in every way each drop

painted on by a master's brush

barry edgar pilcher
inishfree writers

A Hole in the Sky

The sun peeps down
Through a hole in the sky,
Golden rays reaching,
Like shining rods, into the sea,
As if the last remnants of the day,
Reluctant to part,
Reach out with dazzling fingertips
To hold onto the world.

Soon, in wondrous, radiant glory
The sky will fill with fire,
A grand farewell,
A curtain call
To end this glorious day.

The Little Hermit Crab

I am a little hermit crab
vulnerable and shy
I'd like to stay and talk awhile
But must away and hide.
My home, you see, is moveable,
though constantly I try
to stay in one place for a time,
I can't —
          here comes the tide.

It's really very difficult
to make a friend or two.
How can I when I never stop,
I'm always on the move.
My home is in a winkle shell,
At least, it is today,
But come tomorrow, who can say,
A whelk is where I'll be?

235

One day I found an urchin shell
Empty on the strand,
Pink and palely delicate,
I fancy very grand.
I crawled inside to take a look,
My winkle on my back,
And for a while I stayed and dreamed,
But no, t'was not for me.

I need a place where I can hide,
To curl up safe inside,
Where no big predator can reach
and snatch me from within.
I carry an anemone
Stuck firmly to my back,
And when the enemy in near
Anemone attacks!

I scuttle in and out of pools
And run along the shore
I'm really very busy
And I cannot stop for more.
I'm a busy little hermit crab,
Vulnerable and shy,
I'd like to stay and talk awhile
But quick!
          Here comes the tide.

Angela Morrey
Inishfree Writers

Roots

An excerpt from *Memories of Dungloe*

*I*n the early 1980s, when I was home on vacation, my daughter Nora and I drove from Dungloe to Burtonport on the old Meenmore Road, and as I was driving along I pointed out one house after another, some occupied, some in ruins, and I described to Nora the family relationship to each one.

The first one that came up was on the right, just as we were leaving Dungloe, and I told her that it belonged to the Greene family and that they were fourth cousins of mine on my mother's side and, therefore, cousins of hers also.

The next house was on the left, and I told her that this one belonged to the McGee family, and that the mother of the family, Roseanne, was a first cousin of mine, on my father's side of the family.

The next house, on the right, was in ruins and it belonged to Big Fanny Boyle, my grandaunt, who was deceased, and the house after that also belonged to another member of the Greene family, another cousin. Then came the ruins of Neil Campbell's house, and I told Nora that Neil had been my grandfather and was the brother of Alec Campbell of Molly Maguire fame, and behind that house was the ruins of another house, which had been owned by Bryan Sweeney, my great-grandfather, also on my father's side.

As we progressed toward Burtonport, I pointed out one house after another which had belonged to, or still did belong to, aunts, uncles, grand-uncles, great-grand-uncles, cousins and I gave a brief description of the family link to each, and Nora listened to all this very quietly. She was only six at the time and finally she had a comment to make, 'Is there any house on this road that didn't belong to a relative of ours?'

I laughed at her and told her that there were many, but even so if I were to track the family back far enough I would find some sort of relationship, even if it were just tenth cousin.

"Over a period of ten or twelve generations everybody in this area has some kind of family connection, because most people here marry people from around here, so the odds are that over a long time distant cousins are marrying distant cousins and that's why everybody is related."

From time to time I would have these discussions with Nora and Padraic about their relatives and they would display some interest for a time, but if I would talk too much about roots, they would get obviously bored and I would terminate the conversation.

I understood the lack of interest of my children in family history because when I was their age, my father used to talk all the time about the history of our family, and it had been very difficult for me to maintain an interest in what he was talking about since he went into such detail about all the various branches of the family.

It seemed very important to him, however, that I understand who my ancestors were, and who my cousins were, and he never tired of pointing out to me various buildings and slices of land connected with our family's history.

Once he brought me to the ruins of Doe Castle, the ancient stronghold of the MacSweeneys, a Gaelic sept, and he told me that we were descended through his mother's side with the last MacSweeney chieftains who ruled from there.

I walked with him through the deserted and desolate structure that was roofless and inhabited by crows and ravens and tried work up some feelings about my family ties with this place, but felt nothing; and even when I touched the building blocks that had been placed there five hundred years before, I still felt nothing.

In later years, a cousin of my father's, General Joe Sweeney was elected Chieftain of the MacSweeneys at a clann reunion held at Doe, which was attended by MacSweeneys from all over the world, including a Spanish count; and although I could have been part of this gathering I did not go because I would still not have made an emotional link with the MacSweeneys of the fifteenth century or work up any enthusiasm for their glory days.

Once, while on a visit to Inishfree, I sat outside my grandfather's house, which is located on high ground at the centre of the island and has a commanding view of Dungloe Bay and the surrounding areas within ten miles of Dungloe. As I sat there surveying the scene on a beautiful summer afternoon I realized that I had within my view terrain that my ancestors had lived and died on for 500 years or more.

Half a mile away, near the beach was the house of Bryan Gallagher, my great-grandfather, who had moved there from Aranmore in 1850, and beyond the shoreline, three miles away was Aranmore, where Bryan Gallagher, and his father Patrick Gallagher, and his (my great, great, great-grandfather) Timothy Gallagher had lived and died, and also in Aranmore were the Greenes, one of whom married Bryan Gallagher, and I could track the Greenes all the way to 1750.

On the mainland, within sight, was a hillside named Cnoc na Garaigh (the hillside of the sheep) where a dozen generations of Campbells had lived.

They had no way of knowing it at the time, but a daughter of Tim's — Mary — would marry a nephew of Alec Campbell's 35 years later and the Gallaghers and the Campbells would have family ties — the ties that bound me to both clans.

The landscapes that surrounded Dungloe and the mountains that circled the town were clearly visible from Inishfree, and on this terrain the Greenes, Wards, Sweeneys, Boyles, Dohertys, Gallaghers and O'Donnells who had been my ancestors had left their mark on the countryside in the form of abandoned dwellings and ancient houses reduced to a heap of stones.

Over the centuries, as I tracked back in my family tree, I found family roots on all of those hillsides, meadows and mountains that were clearly visible to me as I sat outside Tim Gallagher's house in Inishfree.

I do not know whether it is important or not to have this knowledge of who my ancestors were and if it adds anything to the quality of my life.

However, it does not do any harm to have this knowledge, and I have passed it on to my daughter with the same enthusiasm that my father passed it on to me, and it will be up to her to pass it on to her children — or, if she so chooses, let the memories of our ancestors drift off into the dark void of the past.

Patrick Campbell
Inishfree Writers

239

Sleep Now, the Storm has Passed

For Valerie

Sleep now, the storm has passed
I whisper through the ether
Down the soft, velvet dark
Your tears in flood have dissipated
The body's wrenching eased
Sleep now in the cradle
Of this night's hush. Its gentle breeze

Trouble your scared and sacred self no more
The whole shooting-match
Has trundled drunkenly back across
A rent sky, to the elemental north
Hoarse with shouting
Spent as a damp squib
You've come through, a little thinner
Yet you live

Sleep now, the storm has passed
Thunder did not crack your heart
Nor lightning strike you dead
It only seems that way
Be still, be calm
On the prow of your soporific bed
The contrite wind and I
Blow the eternal kiss
Whisper love's sweet narcotic

I offer a mantra:
That which passes, passes like clouds
(write my name on rice-paper,
          throw it to the wind and see!)
Let fall, as you oftimes did your dress
All screamed, all said and unsaid
And sleep now, the storm is past;
No longer overhead.

Royce Harper
Newtownabbey Writers' Group

Andrea Returns

*J*n 1821 John and Elizabeth Dudgeon left Inishfree for America. In 1997 (176 years later), Andrea, their great, great, great granddaughter, returned.

She couldn't have been blamed for imagining she had entered a time-warp!

Three people on a little piece of land in the ocean pushing wheelbarrows — the only wheels on the island, and the only means of transporting anything.

My neighbours, the Morreys, and I had stopped to have a rest, when we noticed a young woman walking hurriedly from the pier, buffeted by the strong winds. It wasn't a day to expect any visitors, and we waited.

She said she was a descendant of the island — the Dudgeon family — and hoped we would be able to show her her ancestors' home, and was told to ask for Margaret Duffy. I introduced myself, and said I would be delighted, and in the short time tried to tell her as much history as I could. I also suggested she have a talk with our local historian, Packie Bonner, in Dungloe.

It was such a pleasure meeting Andrea. Unfortunately she had to rush away — her mother and relative were anxiously waiting in stormy conditions in the small boat at the pier.

It was decided to show one of the precious letters in this anthology. I know Andrea will return to Inishfree.

Dudgeon Family History

John Dudgeon was born in 1792 in Ireland. His father was Richard Dudgeon and (possibly) Sarah Grant. John married Elizabeth McConnell of Inishfree on February 18, 1817. In 1821, John and Elizabeth Dudgeon left Inishfree, Ireland for America. John's brothers Richard, Guy, Thomas and Gale Dudgeon, as well as their mother, all came, too. They all settled in Amsterdam, near Steubenville, Ohio. John and Elizabeth

241

brought their daughter, Mary Ann, with them, and left their ill 4 year old son William in Ireland. William died the year after they left.

John died on September 6, 1937. In later years, Elizabeth went to Ripley West Virginia with her grown son, James. Richard went to Wisconsin, Gale to Illinois. Guy. Dudgeon remained in Amsterdam. All of them have many descendants in those locations.

The original John and Elizabeth had seven or eight more children after arriving in the United States. One of those children was James, who was born on June 17, 1825. James married Harriet Slaughter in 1860. One of their children was Elizabeth Dudgeon who married Louis Wetzel McKown. This couple had a farm in Ripley, West Virginia. One of their children was Guy Rex McKown, who was my grandfather.

It is through this line that the enclosed letters were passed. The letters were written to John and Elizabeth Dudgeon from their relatives in Inishfree and Rutland during 1822 through 1828.

January, 1997 AJ Bhatt

Dudgeon Family Diary

Eclipse on the Sunday, September 7, 1820
John Dudgeon was married to Elizabeth McConnell the 18th of February, 1817
William Dudgeon was born December 18,1817
Mary Anne Dudgeon was born October 22,1819
Alexander Dudgeon was born October 22nd, 1823
Richard Dudgeon was born June 17, 1825
James Dudgeon was born June 17, 1825
Sarah Dudgeon was born September 25,1827
Jane Dudgeon was born April 5,1830
John Dudgeon was born March 23,1832
Charles Dudgeon was born July 5th, 1834
Guy Dudgeon was born July 5th, 1834
Margaret Dudgeon was born July 24,1837
John Dudgeon died 6th of September
Sarah Dudgeon died May 16th, 1832
John Dudgeon died June 3rd, 1838
Margaret Dudgeon died the September following
Guy Dudgeon died September 3, 1839
Alexander Dudgeon died September 19th, 1852

January 24, 1997
5541 Radcliffe Road
Sylvania, Ohio 43560

Mrs. Margaret Duffy
lnishfree
Burtonport
Co. Donegal
Ireland

Dear Mrs. Duffy,

Thank you for your lovely letter. It was a wonderful pleasure to hear from you.

As I think back to our meeting, I am amazed at how fortuitous it was. I have dreamed for many years about the possibility of actually visiting the Inishfree of my ancestors. It was a thrill to actually be there and 'walk where they walked '. But the greatest luck was meeting you and learning about the house and the history of Inishfree. Many thanks for your graciousness in showing me the house and sharing the feel of the island with me.

Unfortunately, the time we were able to spend in Ireland this time was very short. Also, my mother was not well while we were there which made the visit to Inishfree very brief. I look forward to an extended visit to the area — hopefully this summer.

We did have the good fortune to also meet Mr. Bonner who shared with us his wealth of knowledge about Inishfree and the Dudgeons. I will be sending him the same copies that I am sending to you. I am sure that you both can fill in many of the gaps for us.

Our family came to the United States from Inishfree in 1821. As I indicated to you, we have several letters that these ancestors received from their relatives on Inishfree and Rutland. Enclosed are copies of those letters and the transcriptions for your information. Also enclosed is a page with some background information about our Dudgeon family, as we are able to piece it together. (My mother and I have been working on this for almost 25 years.) I look forward to discussing it with you.

Just to give you a little knowledge about me, I am married to a professor and have two sons — one junior at the University of Notre Dame and the other a freshman at Princeton University. I am a business executive for a US chemical company and work with my mother on our family history for a hobby. We explore the lineage but are most interested in understanding the places and times in which our ancestors lived. The Inishfree story has always been the most captivating for us. Thanks to you and the others of County Donegal, it is now coming to life.

I will keep in touch with you and let you know if it is at all possible for me to return — if not this year, then certainly by next year. Again, many thanks for your interest and hospitality. I look forward to meeting you again.

Warmest regards,

Andrea McKown Bhatt

Mrs. Dudgeon
Crops Creek Township
State of Ohio
America
Inishfree June 6th, 1822

Dear Sister,

I am sorry to have the sorrowful tale to tell of Brother William. Owen O'Donnell that was in Capt. Hanlon's; ould Peter Dougan, Fargil O'Donnell; and Meal Mary's son, young Billy Duffy, left this island on Saturday about two of the clock with the intention to fish in Trawenagh, it being New Year's Eve. It was the turn of ebb. Peter was their skipper. There was none of the boys against going in over the Bar on [the] Marameelan and Cladagh na dTonn side. Their conductor went as he thought fit. They never found to there came a tremendous sea that broke on them and filled the boat to the foot-sparring. When William was going or after rising to go back to steer the boat with the oars, the second sea came and took him and the three oars out, and then the boat was unmanageable. Brother called twice: 'Boys, dear, don't leave me'. He remained a long time over water though he could not swim and much encumbered with double clothing on. The boat was upset in some time after close to the shore, and Owen, Peter and Fargle shared the same [fate] as poor William. The evening was good. Brother was about half a mile from the shore and was got shortly after night and was waked in Neal O'Donnell's of Marameelan that night.

We got no word until after breakfast time Sunday, next morning. He was got about a mile from where he was put out of the boat. He was rubbed along the sand slightly, with a cut on his forehead and finally we kept him two nights in Innisfree.

Many a time your son blamed you and Tedda that did not come up from Rutland to see Big Min that was drowned with a big load of hay. Your son departed this life the twenty-second of May last. He had good health to about Hallow Eve and then he began to get a cough. He was bad with it before he took his flight. You may be thankful to the Almighty for calling him. He was thirteen days that he lived on drink — only what was lifted [once?] on a tay spoon. He is buried along with Brother William. The last words that he spoke was: 'Look at him there'. He was asked who was it. He said: 'Big Min.'

Tom Dudgeon is to be superannuated on twenty pounds per annum. It is wonderful you did not answer the letter that Tom sent[you(?)]. Tell Sall Dudgeon to write and mention whether she lost her clothes or if only you and John's clothes was lost.

My mother, sisters and brother joins [in] their love to you and family.

Yours to death.

Alex McConnell

P.S. Remember me to all my friends, well wishers and auld neighbors from the Rosses in that country. I am in a hurry. At the kiln this fine day as warm as it is there. This [letter] goes with Johndy Grawney (Ghráinne). The potatoes is going from Scotland to Connaught this year.

T.O.T.A.L.!

*W*e regretted the necessity for it. We were left with no choice. TOTAL! The 'Turn Off The Ads League'.

In *passionate*, earnest defence of 20th Century civilization we formed the *organisation that was to spread throughout the planet,* the organisation that challenged bureaucracy, defending the freedom of the individual. From a small group in West Donegal we grew to shake the power of governments. We were TOTAL.

The 'Turn Off The Ads League'.

It certainly started in a minor key. Our object was to eradicate the advertisements that ruined films on television. The more popular the film the more it was spoiled by gratuitous interruption at quarter-hour — or even ten-minute — intervals. After the third barrage of banal repetitious appeals to purchase soap powder, cereal and chocolate bars even the hardiest of us gave up watching classic cinema and retired to bed with a book.

The first meeting of TOTAL was attended by a mere 12 dedicated remote control addicts. We swore solemnly to use our 'off' buttons at the slightest hint of approaching Mars Bars purveyors. Nor did we confine ourselves to film breaks. Sports events, quiz contests and chat shows were targeted. Chat shows were invariably preceded by demands that viewers buy cars, ice cream or beer. It was enough to drive the captive audience to drink. The chat show host would then spend 60 seconds grinning inanely, telling of treats to come, before introducing a guitar-wielding group of callow youths, in clothing that would have been refused by refugees from an Ethiopian massacre, yelling into the camera with multi-decibel electronic volume like crazed savages.

Then more commercials. An ad with a modicum of wit would be repeated for years. *Ad nauseum. Classical* music themes were pirated to sell toilet rolls. Chopin plugged chewing gum, Tchaikovsky tea bags and Rimsky-Korsakoff throat lozenges.

No.

Enough.

Stop.

The 'Turn Off The Ads League' was born of such suffering.

Letters to the editors of the *Donegal Democrat, Derry People* and *the Sligo Champion* resulted in our small nucleus expanding at a phenomenal rate. Humanity rose in protest at the brainwashing break. We brandished our remote controls relentlessly. In six months the whole country had risen in TOTAL support.

Petrol stations, supermarket chains, breweries, all threatened to withdraw their publicity campaigns in the face of public opinion. Politicians became alarmed, fearing the TV would no longer be viable. They worried about the fate of their overt and covert, blatant and subtle political propaganda programmes.

A Daîl Special Enquiry was commissioned. TOTAL leaders from every county were summoned to attend. The Taoiseach magisterially pointed out that we were threatening the country's economy. We replied by suggesting a compromise, offering to accept an average of 10 minutes' advertising per hour providing it was between and not during programmes. This was not accepted. Advertisers knew that half the population would switch off, possibly forgetting to switch on again, while the other half would have just the right amount of time to make tea. The Mars Bar moguls needed to interrupt, to infiltrate popular appeal television.

Open confrontation ensued — but we had the power to frighten the Government and the money-mad magnates of industry. From Ireland our successful example spread to mainland Europe. Emergency legislation from Brussels proved ineffectual. Only Britain's BBC cornflake-free channels remained relatively immune. American TOTAL groups enthusiastically joined battle. Sitcom canned laughter, selling canned lager, was in danger of extinction. In Australia wholesale unemployment threatened *Neighbours* so-called writers and *Home and Away* so-called actors. Japanese television manufacturers faced bankruptcy. The people of Planet Earth would be brainwashed no longer. There was TOTAL success.

The governments of the world planned reprisals. CIA, FBI, Special Branch agents organised undercover strategies to destroy our TOTAL credibility. They formed 'Protect our Commercial' cults, they presented a solid gold Oscar for the International Ad of the Year at the Hollywood Film Awards. Christian, Buddhist, Methodist and Presbyterian Churches, The Church of Scientology and the Armageddon Suicidalists were encouraged to preach to their followers law and order and TOTAL suppression. Elections worldwide were put into a permanent moratorium when we declared that TOTAL candidates would in future contest them on a platform of 'Ban the Break'.

Of course we were becoming too powerful. We were also too lacking in political chicanery and double-dealing; too honest and too innocent. We were the ordinary men and women in the street. The Establishment had to destroy us.

I am writing this from the seclusion of a remote Pacific island. Two hundred TOTALLY committed idealists are carefully guarded here. We are well looked after. Watched by alert, experienced asylum attendants called 'Guardians of the Deranged'. Governments claim that they have saved the world from 'dangerous deviants'. We have no television sets. The only other inmates of this impregnable institution are Dr Donald Diablo, inventor of the everlasting match and M Aloysius de Poitiers who attempted to patent a motor car which would travel 1000 miles on one gallon of sea water.

Arthur McCaffrey
Inishfree Writers

Afterword
East Meets West

Newtownabbey, Co Antrim Writers
Twin with
Inishfree, Co Donegal

*T*oday is the last day of August, 1998. As I write in my island home on Inishfree, cosy and sheltered, the elements outside, powerfully magnificent, churn the sea, and a gutsy south-west gale chases the rain past my window. A warm, contented feeling steals around my heart — a feeling shared East and West.

Our first cross-border meeting took place in Newtownabbey (26th-27th June, 1998). Initially tentative, spontaneous friendships followed, later to be cemented on Inishfree during weekend 22nd August.

Leaving the pressures and influences of the outside world behind on the mainland, the sea breeze deftly wafted any remaining worries or fears over the waves, out to sea. Landing at the pier, the sun shone and Inishfree welcomed.

Our Writers' Workshop was successful and enjoyable. Our time together happy and memorable. With warmth, dignity and respect prevailing any differences between us paled into insignificance by the joy of discovering how much we had in common.

With the beauty of sand, sea, sky and islands around us, we were also keenly aware how fortunate and privileged we were to be able to form our friendships amidst the splendour of God's creation.

Some comments made by our Newtownabbey friends in the guest book speak volumes —

Peaceful hands shake peaceful hands.

There is no beauty like that of Ireland and nowhere so idyllic as its islands.

Lovely colours and textures, fine hospitality. We are blessed to be here.

Remember those when forgotten.

250

This is the stuff of dreams, surrounded by history. How can you not be inspired?

Warm hospitality, beautiful Inishfree. I feel a poem coming on. I can believe this island draws you back.

My past years on Inishfree influenced my life. The original islanders were like one big family.

There was great harmony, one caring for the other. In 1963, I was privileged to become part of this family when I married and came to live on the island.

There were about 50 inhabitants, a school and a post office. At that time the islanders were still untouched or influenced by the outside world. They didn't require a university degree to know how to live in peace — they instinctively knew. With their faith in God, respect for themselves and each other, goodwill automatically followed. Their unparalleled hospitality and ability to reach out especially towards visitors and strangers impressed me greatly, but most of all I loved the aura of 'lightness' created by their sense of fun and laughter.

I always felt the rest of the world could have learned so much from them.

Alas! that era is over, but our cross-border friendships have their blessings. Their spirit and goodness will give us strength.

With God's help 'Our Bridge' will have enduring strength, to be crossed over with a lilt to our step in the knowledge that neighbourly love, loyalty and laughter awaits
East and West.

Margaret Duffy
Inishfree Writers

Who the contributors are...

Margaret Ardill
A housewife, lives in Jordanstown with her husband and three teenage sons. A former civil servant, she has been writing for about ten years, mostly short stories. She was the winner of the Downtown Radio short story competition in 1997.

Sarah Barrett
Born in Belfast, Sarah is a retired civil servant, married with three children and eight grandchildren. Her hobbies include computing, gardening, photography, genealogy, playing the organ, collecting memorabilia. Sarah is a member of North of Ireland Historical Society and World Vision. She began to write fiction in 1997.

Kathleen Rodgers Brady
Born 20th February 1936. Parents Daniel and Isabella Rodgers. Married Andrew 8th August 1958. Children Anne-Marie, Paul Kathleen and Andrew. Educated St Nicholas Primary, St Mary's Senior Secondary, Bathgate, Craiglockliart Teachers' Training College, Edinburgh Occupation: Primary School Teacher. Other writing: Poems published in local newspapers. Unpublished: short stories and children's poems. Kathleen has always loved music and poetry. Since retiring and coming to live in Donegal, I feel compelled to write about people and places here. Address: Leabgarrow, Arranmore Island.

Maureen Browne
Born 1958 in Glasgow to Donegal parents has 4 brothers and 4 sisters. Now living in the Rosses, Co Donegal with husband Jack and 3 daughters Emer, Aine and Blathnaid. Joined the Inishfree Writers' Group in Spring 98 after doing a workshop on creative writing where I was overwhelmed by people's need and joy of listening and sharing. I feel privileged to be involved with the cross border peace initiative.

Patrick Campbell
Born in Dungloe Co Donegal, his mother a native of Inishfree Island. Patrick Campbell now resides in New Jersey USA. He is married with one daughter, Nora. He has published four books and is involved in the making of several Irish-American historical network films. He is also working with them on his controversial book the *Molly Maguire Story*.

Margaret Duffy

In 1963 Margaret Duffy married islander Patsy Duffy. Inishfree became her home It was a happy island, the 50 inhabitants like one big family. Their daughter Mairead was born into this unique and harmonious atmosphere. Years between were spent in London and Belfast But the 'pull' of Inishfree was strong and Margaret returned 8 years ago to live permanently once more to enjoy the beauty and tranquillity of the island and renew her creative interests.

Nora Eagleson

Born, reared and schooled in Inishfree Island, Co Donegal. As oldest of family of 5, deeply regretted having to leave school aged 11 to keep house for father on mother's untimely death at 39. Now resident permanently in Scotland since 1946. Visits Donegal on regular annual basis and at 72 hopes to continue for many more years yet.

Stephanie Handley

Stephanie was born in Bristol in 1936, and was convent-educated. Retired to Ireland with husband, Colin, and Havana cat, Ruari, in 1997, all three enjoy touring holidays in the campervan. Stephanie is presently the secretary of Dungloe Guild of the ICA. Stephanie is a fan of Daniel O'Donnell, and enjoys meeting with and writing to other fans.

Royce Harper

Royce has been writing poems and lyrics since 1975. Discovered by a BBC producer when performing his work at Club One (organised by Rathcoole Musicians' Workshop). He has read and performed poems and satires on BBC Youth programmes (N.I.) and Radio Ulster. His first collection, *The Giant's Breath*, was published in 1984. His second book *The Action of Waves*, is out this year from Lapwing Press.

Bill Hatton

A teacher of English, with four sons. Currently looking for a publisher for *Spricks*. Interested in Ulster-Scots culture.

Jim Johnston

Married, father of two boys. Works in integrated education.

Gerry McAuley

Born in Belfast, he now lives in Newtownabbey with his wife and daughter and their pet labrador Zak. As a rock musician during the Sixties and Seventies he travelled extensively throughout Great Britain and Europe. He has written several short stories and many poems, none of which, so far, have been published.

Anna McCann

Anna McCann lives in St Agnes' Parish, Andersonstown. She has been involved with parish music, production of a magazine and with the handicapped.

Arthur McCaffrey

Has lived in Falmore since 1991. Family from Belfast, has worked in theatre in Dublin and newspapers in the English Midlands. Spends his time gardening, writing and reading — and making out quiz questions and trying to solve crossword puzzles.

Valerie Maher

Born in Belfast in 1943, Valerie now lives in Randalstown, the mother of five children, three boys and two girls - grandmother of eight. Her first book, *Walls of Glass*, was her autobiograhy, published by Pretani Press. Her second book, *Sarah's Gate*, is an Ulster comedy, published by Brookland Press.

Angela Morrey

A qualified Healing/Shiatsu practitioner; is now enjoying the time to write and also create colourful collages inspired by the ever-changing colours and moods of the island and the elements.

Gilbert Morrey

Took early retirement about four and a half years ago and moved to Inishfree, where he enjoys a healthy outdoor life. Apart from writing, he spends his time gardening and ruminating on the meaning of life.

Brian Mullan

Brian works in various media. He has worked abroad for Disney and Warner Bros.

Aileni Calonyddaear Noyle

Became hopelessly infected with the writers' bug in the mid-1960s. He quickly discovered there was more to communicating than met the eye. Writing and illustrating for science fiction fanzines such as Robert Holdstock's *Macrocosm* provided a valuable testing ground. After sixteen years as a radiographer, ACN went to Art College, thence to freelance photography and journalism. He contributed articles to *Bike* Magazine and to *Ad Astra*. Founded a Writers' Group in Llanelli. Over the years AGN has fruitlessly bounced several novels around the marketplace of agents and publishers. The optimist fool is just completing yet another.

ACN, wife Meri and five children came to Inishfree in September 1990, fleeing life on a council estate in Wales. The story *Rose* had its origin on 1st March 1996. It was suggested that the cloth upon the table about which the nascent Inishfree Writers gathered, might provide subject matter for their first foray into literary endeavour.

Shirley Ohlmeyer

Born Co Tyrone. Has lived in Northern Ireland, Africa and USA, retired school teacher now living in Cruit.

Maureen O'Sullivan

Born in Wales January 1942, married Donal (originally from

Inishfree) in 1962. Children: Steven, Helen and Mark. Lived in Wales for most of their married life, but returned to Donal's homeland in 1991. Since the late seventies, Maureen has been toying with the idea of writing a book about Donal's mother and family who lived on Inishfree. It wasn't until she returned to Ireland that she started to think seriously about writing it, but needed some support. There was nothing in the area connected with writing so in 1996 decided to form the Inishfree Writers' Group with Aileni Noyle who was living with his family on the island.

barry edgar pilcher

poet musician and mailartist
born in a cottage hospital during
air raid in the london blitz
wrote poetry   played clarinet
from an early age   came to
inishfree to set up a creative base
published world wide small press
and recordings "use all solutions;
do everything!" john cage

Stephen Potts

A consultant paediatric surgeon, he was doctor to the successful first Irish Everest Expedition in 1993. Both his professional work and experiences as a traveller in some of the remote parts of the globe have, along with life in Ulster during the Troubles, formed the basis of his poetry.

Heidi Schulz

Forty-five years old, German, mother of six children, has a deep emotional relationship to Ireland. She has always been fascinated by the nice and bright people the beauty of the country and the endlessness of the ocean. Poems and other art (painting, music) are a way of expressing her emotions and sharing them with other people.

Billy Stewart

Born 1940, married with three children, lived in Newtownabbey for forty years, living at present in north Belfast. Former member of Hammer Writers' Group. Interests are reading, writing, local history, electronics, photography and artwork.

John Threlfall

John is an associate member of Inishfree Writers' Group. His Irish connection is through the Casey and Murphy families of Drogheda. John lives in Barnoldswick on the Lancashire/Yorkshire border. He and his wife, Maureen, make an annual 'pilgrimage' to Donegal, and his skill as writer and critic are invaluable to the Inishfree writers. He is at work on a historical account of the famine times — when his ancestors emigrated to the north of England.

Rhoda Watson

A grandmother, writes for radio, magazines and newspapers. She also presents her work on radio but aspires to write a creed (by author Robert Fulghum):

I believe that imagination is stronger
than knowledge,
That myth is more potent than
history,
That dreams are more powerful
than facts,
That hope always triumphs over
experience,
That laughter is the only cure for
grief.
And I believe that love is stronger
than death.

Iain Campbell Webb

Iain C. Webb was born in Belfast. He has been an active writer for 15 years, his poetry appearing in various Irish literary magazines, and in an anthology of Ulster writers. In 1995 Lapwing Press published a collection of his poems. Last year his work featured in a book celebrating the centenary of Bradford City. He has read at a number of literary festivals, including the Queen's Festival, and has appeared on Radio Ulster, on National Poetry Day. When not writing, Iain pursues his interest in natural history, and the creative mystical traditions. As a wild and wise man once said, 'We are all in the gutter, but some of us are looking at the stars.'